William Bull Wright

Highland Rambles

A Poem

William Bull Wright

Highland Rambles
A Poem

ISBN/EAN: 9783337123352

Printed in Europe, USA, Canada, Australia, Japan

Cover: Foto ©Andreas Hilbeck / pixelio.de

More available books at **www.hansebooks.com**

Highland Rambles:

A POEM.

BY

WILLIAM B. WRIGHT.

———•———

BOSTON:

ADAMS & COMPANY.

25 BROMFIELD STREET.

1868.

STEREOTYPED BY
W. F. BROWN AND CO., BOSTON.

CONTENTS.

DEDICATION.

FROM its Castaly above
Welled a fount of heavenly Love.
Thereof a mortal drank, therein
He cleansed his spirit of its sin.
His eyes caught stronger beams, and tears
Were born to him of deep delight,
A lofty music filled his ears,
And there was offered to his sight
The face of a majestic Soul,
That was not wave nor wind nor light,
But moved and murmured through the whole.

Love is the daintiest thief that ever
Slipped hither out of Paradise.
Nought is so dark but he can sever,
By the fine flashes of his eyes,
The meaning nestling in its heart.
No lore for him too wise or deep,
He can explore with fiery art.
He steals from the coy rose asleep
The dreams she would to none impart,
And ere the river can hasten by,
He will its darting god espy.

And without Love may none unlock
The secret temple-gates of God.
Though mazes mingle, phantoms mock,
Love has no fear, he finds a road,
Smites prison'd fountains from the rock,
And wears a full-orbed faith that, beaming
On every form of truth or seeming,
Finds nothing with so hard a face,
But that it keeps some look of grace.
Therefore to LOVE I dedicate
The labors which my hands create.

HIGHLAND RAMBLES.

HIGHLAND RAMBLES.

LOITERING purples droop and dream,
  Languid hazes glimmer,
Tortured by the sultry beam,
  Breezes swoon and meadows simmer.

Tarry longer and receive
  Summer's drowsy potion,
Mope and muse from morn to eve
  Without passion, without motion.

Forth, and snap the cunning fetter;
  Couched in Alpine bower,
Thou shalt have thy senses better
  Where cool-fronted mountains tower.

Hearts of men, 't is said, beat surer
  In their lordly bosoms,
Simpler faiths spring, love flows purer,
  Life comes out in fresher blossoms.

Seeking long in school and temple,
　　Yet no Master's eye
Lights thee to the high ensample
　　Faithful hearts must find or die.

Nature hides in fragrant places
　　Darlings of her own,
Crowns them with her secret graces,
　　Unprofaned by mart or town.

Eyries where the storms are fledged,
　　Tracts with granite shod,
Nurse a race to nature pledged,
　　Homely souls that live with God.

Vagrant feet oft soonest win
　　Shining goals of fate ;
Spindle, doomed thy thread to spin,
　　Doth thine eager hands await.

————◆————

THE first lark shook the dampness from his wings
And throbbed his matins to the flushing morn,
Mildest and latest of a gracious May,
As three strayed spirits, Arthur, Vivian, Paul,
Brushed off the humming swarms of early dreams,
And sprang from beds of pine-boughs underneath
Thick-branching pines.　And Paul, who sought the
　　　　East,

Cried, "Look, the crescent strands her silver keel
Upon the pearly breakers of the dawn."
And Vivian, "Let us climb to yonder peak,
Ere the first rosy ripple break." But he,
Whose wit blew cool as winds from mountain lakes,
Arthur, "Go up. I follow when my brows
Three times are dipped in water." And the three,
Frighting some drowsy pinions yet untrimmed
To the first fancies of the scrupulous beak,
Burst through the mesh of thickets that all night
Had rustled dewy curtains round their slumber,
And rent the leafy woof that sought to screen
The glittering pulses of a spring, and dipped
Into the eddies, and made fresh and cool
Their faces. "Let us touch the gnarry crown,"
Said Paul, "while yet its topmost ridges smoke,
Fresh-tipt by the dank sandal of the night,
And through quaint oriels of the parting mist
Catch swiftly changing pictures of the land."

They glided over bosomed meads, where now
The merle and robin helped the lark to thrill
The brightening cope with pulses of sweet sound,
Shook from the tre-foil half its load of dews,
And won with shout and leap the shaggy spurs
Of the height, and wrestling with the steepness
        gained
The summit, as the first keen lance of the sun
Splintered upon its crest and turned in rout
The trembling vapors. Baiting here their breath,
Stretched at the great paw of a lion-crag,

Silent, and offering to slow-moving airs
Their steaming foreheads, far in front they saw
A surge of misty peaks that rolled in fire,
Touched by the crimson currents from the east,
And marked the morning from a simple maid,
Who strays alone through blushing gardens, change
Into a stately queen who comes with all
Her peers, herself imperial over all.
Below, the ample champaign wore the smiles
Of two auroras ; one above in heaven,
And one the shining season half-way orbed.
Fresh tints upon a thousand meadows gleamed,
Where with her rod the month struck node and spray,
Unsealing founts of bloom.   Majestic floods
Of verdure swept across the wrinkled plains
In polished waves, with drifts of purple foam,
Or rippled up to kiss with vivid lips
The hard feet of the mountains.   East and west
The multitudinous knoll upleaped and laughed,
Crowned with white orchard - garlands, thick with
        flower,
Whose boughs sustained with slumberous ease their
        freights,
Like milky swans that dream in placid waves,
Their plumes stirred oft by dalliance of the wind.
The herded granges sparkled brown or white,
As barn and dwelling chanced.   A happy land !
Laden with splendors of the perfect May,
Heralding with initial pomp the march
Of the great queen to come with larger gifts,
A mellower ether and more pregnant suns.

But now the valleys murmured of the day.
In struggle from the rosy bands of sleep
The hamlets stirred, and silver shafts of smoke
Mounted to heaven from the ivied homes
Sown in the quiet furrows of the land ;
Long heired of pastoral Peace, whose haunts were
      thick
For slumber and the piping of his loves.
The lusty cackle from the granges blended
With lowings and with bleatings faint, and all
The subtle rhetoric of happy sounds
The valleys love to fondle in their breasts.
Idyls, sweet-luted from innumerous groves,
Filled the wide air with unexpressive notes
Fresh from the lips of nature in her prime.
Unto the broadening splendor of the skies
Surrendered wholly, all were mute till Paul
With softest accents sang a little song,
Pattering the crags with tender drops of rhythm,
That seemed a space to smooth their savage frown.

  The hand of morn is Dian-cool,
    Her maiden brows serenely bright ;
  But from her eyes mayst quaff thee full
    Of rich, ambrosial light.

  The fretful heart lies glad and still,
    Charmed through and through with utter bliss ;
  The lordly mind forgets his will,
    So pure her beauty is.

Who looks upon her is made wise;
  More than his mystic Vedas tell,
With holy awe the Brahmin's eyes
  Read in her miracle.

Wouldst sing the gift her eye-beams bring,
  Sweet be thy melodies and strong;
The gift her eye-lids keep, wouldst sing, —
  That were Apollo's song.

But their sweet moods were broken, as he closed,
By the slow advent of a foot that pressed
A ledge that neighbored. Straightway all arose,
Startled to sudden reverence by one,
Noble in mien, though bowed beneath his years.
Leaning upon a gnarled staff he seemed
Some fragment of an antique world, a sage
Fit to have fostered kingliest hearts, and shown
Beauty and truth to a heroic age ;
Sublime Prahláda wandering sole at dawn,
Or Saturn crowning an Italian hill
In the golden prime. From ample brows serene
White locks flowed back in streams, and snow-
      fringed eyes,
Wherein a hundred dewy Aprils slept,
Shone earnestly, the beacons of a soul
Accustomed to adore. The signs august
Of eldest wisdom furrowed either cheek,
And a perpetual heaven of kindliness
Dwelt on his features. While abashed they gazed,
He smiled, and said :

"My sons, I welcome you.
'T is mine to welcome, for meseems I read
A softer clime upon your cheeks, not masked
With our rude bronze, and in your eyes I find
Perplexéd mirrors of unwonted scenes.
But days remote from man, a charm, perchance,
That never quite forsakes the prospect hence,
Have taught my feet these paths for many years,
Morning or evening. The kind chance that weds
Our hours of travel, giving to my ears
Your Memnon utterance, doubtless purposes
Closer acquaintance. And I think the Morn,
So young and fair, has sown the self-same forms
Of beauty and of thought in either breast,
To make us, each to know the other, ripe."
"I thank the chance," said Paul, "whate'er it be,
Gracious, it seems, that crosses here our paths
Upon the glowing headlands of the dawn."
And Vivian cried, "Three half-blown pedants we,
New-fledged from Academic nests, not yet
Full masters of the wing. Some vacant months
We slip the Sisyphean weight of books,
And sweep our thoughts of all scholastic dust
And esoteric breathings of the schools ;
Bathing our souls in highland valleys, shade
And sunlight, treading with monastic feet
The sylvan aisles and loud oracular seats
Of nature. We are fugitive, in part,
From the tumultuous stress of city cares,
And shun the sudden fangs of lurking plagues."
Then Arthur with a seeming-careless palm

Caught up the distaff of discourse, and said,
" We steer not for the Golden Fleece, nor some
Atlantis sunk from sight of men, but fling
Free sheets to any vagrant breeze that asks,
Or drift on random tides from isle to isle.
I hold it much too wanton.   Better far
Some practiced pilot sat astern to shape
The voyage, lest we wholly fail of port.
But, Sir, it seems a marvel that you bear
So lightly this great burthen of your years."

And the Sire said, " Not mounting from the fields
Have I attained this eminence.   For that
Scarce now abides enough of youthful force.
The sinews slacken and the limbs that fought
Gladly aforetime with laborious tasks
Are withered.   This sere age hangs from its branch
A sapless stem, which the next wind will snap.
See you the wrinkle on the shaggy cheek
Of yonder mountain ?   There a cataract,
Sweet-voiced, forever tames the sullen crags
To its blithe moods, and birds of liveliest throat
Pour all day long unfailing founts of glee
From grove and thicket.   There a meek cot peeps
Beneath the mossy eaves of sheltering cliffs,
Through pleasant arbors native to the spot.
There have I dwelt these many years and touched
A world above the jarring world of men."

" If you will pardon curious eyes that pry,"
Said Vivian, " from untempered youth, in part,

And somewhat from a rule we have, to probe
Adventure to the quick, we would be taught
The reason of your solitude that wears
A front so strange.   For we have learned the lore
Of action duteous unto social ends,
Drawing its argument from social needs."

And the grey man put forth a hand that blessed
The moving world below him, as he said,
" Majestic are the feet of him who marches
With patience in the ordered ranks of men ;
Leagued to his kind by bands of faith and love,
Sharing with them the burthen and the wrong,
Yet striking with them unto aims of worth.
But souls are born to whom the blaring mart
Of the world affords no custom ; souls that hear
Monitions which they know.   To such it seems
Better in frozen silence to refrain,
Better the dormant impulse, lifeless palm,
Than to be married to unsteadfast things.
For me, my heart is in the village there,
Milk-white ; the cradle where my youth was rocked,
First sipped the honeyed dews of life and read
Fondly the glorious features of the hills.
There bloom some branches of my stock, a son
And a rare flower, his daughter.   And the breath,
The fragrant breath of filial tenderness,
Mounts to my tranquil shades.   Often they come,
Laden with choicest courtesies and gifts,
And one day I will go to them to die.
While the conducting years led up my feet

From gardens of quick-budding youth to slopes
Of manhood, some deep-hearted ponderings
Grew in me, visions of a dawn to break
Within me with a splendor of its own.
The future pressed upon me with strange thoughts
That wrought like fire. Long stung by stirring hints,
Shot down from stars or whispered by the earth,
Or inly prompted by the restless mind,
I caught swift glimpses of a fleeting god
Half-seen, and touching with elusive step
That bursting prime ; a near mysterious sense
Of somewhat nobler than the phantom world
Of eye and ear, a good not to be compassed.
And when young Phosphor muffled his pale ray
Behind a skirt of saffron cloud, or when
The Great Bear loitered o'er the northern crests,
I soothed the feverous heart with wanderings
Through these inviolate solitudes. Therefrom
Blossomed a dearness which ensuing years
Have ripened into passion. And my hearth,
When death had stolen away its ornament,
Making the wife's chair vacant, pierced me so
With memories that haunted every nook,
I passed the staff of office to my son,
The labor and the mastery, and sought
My cottage in the crevice of the hills.
But ere the fierce day packs our soles with lead,
Will ye not fare with me an hour and taste
Some matin cheer beneath my boughs, and hear
The brook make merry ? "

Gladly they set forth,
Spell-drawn by wonder and the mystic sanction
Of his seraphic eyes whose lightnings mild
Held all of heaven molten, and by hearts
Prophetic of some blessing linked to him.
In slow descent by gently sloping paths,
Threading the passes, climbing here and there,
They moved, and spied a winding gorge that roared
Unto a brook, in wildest lion-sport
Tossing his angry foam from rock to rock ;
Mad as a colt that, bursting his low bound
Flings high his swelling mane, and in pursuit
Of greener pastures weaves with supple grace
The motions of his beauty.   By its side
The glossy verdure flowed in noiseless stream,
Broke to a thousand gentle rivulets,
Trickled down dewy clefts and peeped in cool
And fountained coverts sprinkled through the crags.
They paused to view the sinuous vales below ;
Trim fields with buttercup and crowfoot pied,
Dark belts of wood with pale green streaks between,
Bright flecks of light dappling the distant slopes,
And where through a far throat a village spire
Flashed, and beyond a sheen of sunny waves.
Entering the gorge they met a lawn inurned,
Walled round with sudden steeps that dripped with
        moss.
To this sweet refuge stolen from tedious flights,
The cradled zephyrs rocked themselves asleep,
Or sporting baby-breezes dipped on wings,
That only faintly shook the slumberous air,

From bush to bush, low-prattling.   On the right
A monstrous willow drooped in solemn state,
Bathing her golden hair in lucid pools
Piled up with foam.   And half-way steeped in shade,
Here couched a ruddy heifer drowsily,
Perfect in delicate curve of neck and horn,
Covering her chestnut globes of mellow light
Momently with dusk lids, the while her throat
Throbbed through its sleekiness with change of cuds,
And mixing shades chequered her polished flanks.
They crossed to where the cot slyly retired
Through double-folded depths of foliage,
Withdrawn within the cool frown of the cliff.
And here a score of downy throats were oped
With silver welcome ; ditties of all notes
From robin clear to tiny-piping wren.
On rustic benches shagged with bark of pine,
They sat and cooled their eyes against the green
And peaceful leafiness of mingled boughs.

Then Vivian whose young soul yet fought with mists,
And ever seeking, sought not aimlessly
Nor with sure knowledge, spake with earnest tones
Half passionate, as if his heart were sad :
"O softer than Arcadian lawns or beds
Of richest clover where the summer's cheek
Roses in slumber, unto weary eyes
And hearts that sicken in the blatant crowd,
These flinty peaks would feel !   Here through calm
        days
To ponder on existence and fulfil

The measure of full manhood, to achieve
Vision, most blessed gift of God, and peace,
This it were well to do.   Hushed hours of rapt
Perception, keenly sundering the clouds
That darken, tranquil pulses that maintain
The intellect in equal poise to weigh
What Silence with a million hands would bring,
And the most self-less heart of love that feels
Tenderest confessions of the flower and star,
All these would flock with golden tribute round,
And help the building hands of man to base
On rock, whose roots strike to the centre, firm,
His life, which battering siege of worldliness,
And all the leaguing doubts that shake the mind,
Might waste their pith against."
                    Then Arthur ; he
Who better loved to dash his daring heart
Against the front of hardiest enmities,
To dally with the bristling crests of the Deep,
Or boldly touch the stops of enterprise,
Than court the sweets of moods contemplative
By vigils and by solemn musings lone :
"Medicinal, no doubt, it seems to men
Agued with fear, perplext by shallow tongues,
The scrannel chorus of a wildered time,
To take cool-witted Silence by the hand
And learn of her.   This is not wholly loss,
Foregoing not for aye the benison
Of civic toil and knitting of like spirits.
But men have grown love-mad with loneliness,
Browsed on the brakes and fondly yielded up

Their root-fed souls to starry promptings, coy
Of mortal amity and swift to plunge
Like otters into darkness.   Is the soul
Incapable of height unless exiled
From fellowship, centred in blasted tracts?
O why so dainty?   Is it better thus
To slip the burden than to toss it high
With hope renewed?   Tame not the foot ordained
To sport with cliff and barrier, thorn and shard,
To velvet pacings in ambrosial groves.
Who lives to dream, propped upon flowery peaks,
Nursed down by fondling phantasms of the mind
From virile sinews to the thewless pulp
Of infants, or to point with languid scorn
At the low haunts and seething marts of men?
Life is not life that is not daringly
Plucked from the open jaws of angry fate.
Sequestered from the onset and the shock
Of rude antagonisms, all dedicate
To buoyant leisure and to sylvan thoughts
Who may not wear a placid countenance,
Have temperate pulses?   Honor rather him
Who keeps his soul serene when all the state
Rocks to the civic tempest ; mindful yet
Of hope and duty.   And I most revere
The man who to the final verge of all
Drags slowly weary steps, sprinkled with stains
Of travel, scarred with many wounds, sure signs
Of long enduring toil.   For me, my arms
May wither to the trunk but they shall strive
To leaven and to knead the dough of the time."

And Paul flung out a loud, ironic laugh :
" Certes, young Alexander — Tamerlane,
I see the peoples flock to kiss your rod,
The viziers and the hoary senates kneel.
Bestride your world and ride it round the sun.
But if you stoop before my stoic tub
To bar my sunlight with your purple, mark,
I blind your royal eyes with musty straw."
" Not Alexander, then Diogenes,"
Said Arthur, laughing.   And the Father smiled
To see the sparks leap from their crossing blades,
And looking upon Arthur, said, " My son,
I blame you not.   I love the fearless eye,
The bounding pulse, the heart that like a steed
Springs unto action.   These if wisely trained
And taught the equal yoke of steadfast law,
May strain the world ahead a notch or two.
But wisdom first must quell their lawless ramp,
Must tame their scorn and gird their might with
          meekness,
Till Love, the elfin maid, may curb their foam
With reins of gossamer.   So shall they strive
Co-operant with what is just and good,
Not marring."
                  Vivian then ; his cheek flushed through
With transient shame, " Arthur, not all may boast
Sinews that never quail, but lightly poised,
Dance over dizziest voids.   Lo, you would toss
The babe unweaned and ignorant of his force
To grapple with the tiger-surge of the Deep.
I wander as a child whose young eye, snared

By twinkling lustres in the forest, tempts
His feet to quit his father's door.   All day
He hies, not finding his desire, and sinks
Forlorn, a prisoner of unpitying night,
Trembling at the fierce cries of wolves and pards."

Anon the cottage door upon its hinge
Revolving, showed to all the form of one,
The Oread of the spot, a beauteous maid,
Seeming a strain divine of womanhood
Full-sung to its sweetest ; in her virgin bloom
Appareled as a cloud that wears a scarf
Of iris ; either eyelid burdened low ;
The fine stress of a heart too exquisite.
Bearing a snow-white pitcher in her hand,
A perfect hand and just imbrowned a shade
Caught from the glow of household offices,
With startled glances at the throng, she paused
While thrice a mounting dove would close her wings,
Then like a sunbeam through the leafage slipped.

Paul looked like Eros when he erst beheld
The brows of Psyche.   And the Father said,
"This grandchild is my dearest visitant.
Save when the torrents are too perilous,
Or thawing snows of March go thundering down,
No day of all the year but her glad feet
Climb hither, and her ordering hands control
My scant economy ; or at my side
She turns a chosen page that hits her mood,
Reading, whene'er her heart is touched, aloud,

To have my smiles or tears.   Her soul has fed
From earliest maidenhood upon my words,
Able to frame most cunning reasonings,
Nor lacking in the fine poetic sense.
I find my chiefest solace in her love
And the delightful tale of poesy
Which is her being.   For within her dwells
Clear candor without shade or guile ; a heart
Most sensitive to thoughts of piety ;
Calm hopes that lift her to cerulean homes.
Her spirit sits within her like a star ;
Through all its golden changes it preserves
A law of beauty firm as that which wheels
Wroth Mars or guides the pole of Venus' car,
The gentle law of perfect womanhood,
A soul in love with what is fairest, best.
Ah me, my old lips will not quite forget,
Speaking of her, their trick of eulogy,
So like is she to mine own buried saint."

All heard him reverently, but Paul drank in
His words as thirsty flowers the rain, then said,
"Our maidens yonder wear the magic ring
Of Melusina, choosing to be elves,
Impalaced in an atomy, to whom
Each dew-drop is an orb in heaven afar,
Rather than bear the woman's stature, shield
And spear of ripe Minerva, or than lift
Proudly their foreheads up among the gods.
Scarce would they arch their soft Ledæan necks
To welcome Jove, though widowed of his bolts,

His brows unwrinkled of the thunder-seams,
Unless he staled his godhood to their kind.
And should he summon them to higher themes
Than passion, dalliance, or their own sweet charms,
The purr and purl of sleek wits exquisite,
Yea, though he outlined how his worlds were framed,
Or bared his old Olympic polities,
They 'd straight unruffle all their eager down
And fan their languid lids to sudden sleep.
Fine fairy graces, mimic migniard lores,
Frail arts, like the papilio's purple dust
Brushed from her Psyche-wings at the first touch,
The courtly nothings of luxurious dames,
Lesson too idly her whose stalk should bear
The leaf and blossom of a better time,
Who should nurse kings and bards and mould the
        hearts
Of warriors.   For the woman should move up
The meek and starlike rival of the man,
Colleague in soul through all his climbings-up.
She has her sceptre, equal and not less,
Albeit her lilied realm is far more fair."

Then Arthur, with a comic eye askance,
"Ah recreant, perfidious, without shame,
Unknightly !   Nevermore shall Queen of Love
Crown thee her champion in the sounding lists,
Nor shalt thou tryst to save a maiden's fame.
What if I published this fine railing there
Where oft thy lips composed obeisant vows,
And made their homage smell like Indian gums?

Take heed, lest I proclaim thee what thou art,
And stir the white-armed Mænads to thy doom."

Smiling, the gracious Hermit led them forth,
Where dancing on the edges of a shelf,
The brook reeled, toppled, fell on beds of flint
With showers of shrieks, half laughter and half pain,
And fled among the bosks like one ashamed.
Here on a smooth-faced rock was neatly spread
A cloth that glistened like a patch of snow,
Or some white pennon from the battlements
Of morning ; and thereon were duly ranged
Four liberal bowls of savory milk, and store
Of simple viands, berries of last year,
And, suited to the season, garden-fruits.
" Sit," said the Host, "and feast like true sultans
Of nature, charmed by all her symphonies,
By choirs of timbrels, tabors, lutes and flutes."
And Edith waited on them while they ate.
Long lashes under dark Circassian brows
Curtained the lustrous deeps of lovely eyes,
Blue and as mild as heaven.   Her forehead shone
Pensively broad, Madonna-calm and clear.
And on her lips from time to time was seen
Sweet laughter, luring every soul to love.

Freshened, they strayed, with steps that often paused,
Through thronging arbors, plots of fragrant plants,
Hues wont to pave more lowly wolds, but here
Most winning from their strangeness.   Everywhere
Were visible the motions of a hand

By inner beauty taught and purest love,
That lent new graces. All things seen, they sought
The shady seats, and sitting, talked at ease.
In them the genial power of intercourse
Glowed like a vintage, and they were as friends
Once dear, though sundered long, who now would
        close
With swift and fiery welcome soul to soul.
And when the discourse lulled, the Eldest said,
" You have come hither, as it seems, in part
To loose yourselves from Academic stays,
Unsheathe your spirits from the leaden scales
Of urban manners ; partly, as you said,
To shun the sudden fangs of lurking plagues.
Herein behold some likeness to that famed
Italian exod to Campanian hills
From Florence, plague-struck. Why not model now
Your pastime to the fashion of that prank,
And framing ambush dwellings, tarry here
While three moons come and fill their disks and
        cease ?
For when the fourth is born I will go down
Among my kindred in the vale to die.
Here day will follow cheerful day, each lulled
By some sweet flow of poesy or tale
Choice-culled from garden-spaces of the past,
Fit to beguile the hours of languor, mixt,
As best will suit, with words of wiser weight.
And dipping to the hamlets, we will touch
Our brethren through the daily life and mark
The man among his burdens."

Then they all
Burst forth in loud acclaim, " Lo this is good.
Three moons will we abide, and at the fourth
Go down into the semblance of the world,
And thread the misty alleys of our lives."

II.

WAKES the youth from early bliss
To find the planet sphered amiss :
Perplext through all his purple teens,
Plagues his soul with what it means.

Questions asked of every man,
Questions no man answer can,
Suck the red light from his cheek,
Has no choice but still to seek.
Which is phantom, which is fact,
Which the man's, the Maker's act ?
Lo, behind the rose the thistle,
Just below the god the beast ;
Which is better, bowl or missal,
Cap of fool or alb of priest ?
Lo, the rivers change to rocks,
World-old mountains flow to seas,
Bacchus prays and Phœbus mocks,
Graces startle, Furies please.

And he hears a baleful sound,
Voice of anguish from the ground,
Hears the serpent-hiss of sin
Just without him, just within,

A dread hurtle and a roar,
Chaos tumbling on her shore ;
Voices raised the storm to still,
Babelized against their will ;
Will be saved, can scarcely tell
If from heaven or from hell.

Dawns a morning cool and blue,
Will go forth, undo and do,
Spy the primal cycles through,
Boldly break the eternal seals,
Read the secrets fate conceals ;
Pluck wisdom from the single Soul,
Far-centred ordinance of the whole,
To right the dark earth's prostrate pole.
Falls anon the evening shade,
He drags his soul back sore dismayed,
Brings no boon, has won no token,
Heard no mystic whisper spoken ;
Fledged with large imaginings,
On cliffs of fate has bruised his wings ;
From chasing knowledge round the moon,
Comes home to cobble his own shoon.

———◆———

WHAT hour the white cap of the topmost peak
Flamed like a cresset through Norwegian fogs,
The early Patriarch and his reverent brood
Set forth, the younger hung with wallets puffed

With loaves and dainties for the matin lunch,
And wound with laugh and shout along the rims
Precipitous, and beetling brows that towered
Under the fiery fringes of the dawn,
Westward, and swooped into a vale that slept
In silent circle down betwixt the heights,
Yet high above her sisters of the plain.
Her the great Hills came up to worship, flocked
And from their haughty eminences stooped
To kiss her beauty with too shaggy lips ;
Loosed from their hearts a thousand glittering rills
To bear their messages of love, and placed
The white pearl of a lake upon her breast.
Northward, a monstrous cleft went down and framed,
With ragged borders dark against the morn,
Vast breadths of the world, majestic pérspective,
Under an ample canopy of sky.
The vale here suffered transformation rude.
A throat of horror, never to be closed,
Opened sheer jaws of thunderous abyss,
Piled with the splinters of a shattered sphere ;
Low-diving ledges, shooting spires of cliff,
Gigantic shards and tumbled bowlders, mixt ;
Dread signals of the earth's old agonies.

" Nature can cherish wildest fantasies,"
Said Paul, " but in her moods of gambol hies
To regions of untrodden loneliness.
Such lawless grouping of strange opposites
Confounds the eye with an unguessed delight,
Nor palls, as never wholly reconciled."

"Only the fearless foot," the Master said,
"May track her to her fortresses and spy
Her weird imaginations.   She would put
Her suitors to their duty, shock their faith
With rash surprises, proving if they love.
For him who with a child-like suppliance
Follows her still, she holds in store a good,
A passion that will bless him.   Oft she sheds
Light made intenser by a weight of gloom ;
As you have marked upon the western verge
The level sun pour from a cloudy chink
His unmasked majesty and bathe in light
The world and lower air, while overhead
The leaden vault without a seam of ether
Frowns like a fiend oppressive, doubling so
The beauty he would cancel."
            Arthur then,
"I fancy Thor aforetime came this way,
And overwearied with his walk and wroth,
Flung yonder down his mace in careless spleen,
The while he soothed his limbs there in the vale."
"You angle for conceits ? " said Paul.   "Here's one.
These sun-bleached fragments are the fleshless
      bones
Of Titans sunk beneath the volleyed crags,
Cottus or Steropes or Atlas huge."
"One more," said Vivian.   "The winsome vale
Shadows the white proportions of a nymph,
Exquisite down from brow to slender waist,
Thence metamorphosed like a Nereid maid
That trails her dark sea-coil from sea to shore."

"Ha, ha!" cried Arthur. "Sorely pushed, I trow.
Come, follow me who dares.   For Hades I.
I hear Styx rumble, and I swear to speak
With Proserpine."   And while they stared aghast,
He dangled from a bough and touched a shelf,
And clinging like a lichen now, anon
Bold as a chamois at his play, shot down,
Soon lost to sight.   And all were mute until
A shout as from the heart of Erebus,
Defiant, crag-resounding, bellowed up,
A respite to their fears.   "The grisly hosts
Split their hoarse throats to welcome him," said Paul.
"Good, let him suck the hot malarial steam
Of Acheron alone.   The slope rocks there
Offer light egress when he wills to mount.
For me, I better love Elysian lawns,
Carpets of amaranth and asphodel.
Come, we have Nestor with us, let us find
Some spot embowered where we may recline
And drink the prospect yonder."
　　　　　While they urged
Close scrutiny, their blown Æneas rose
Brow-burning from Inferno, and they sat
Hard by a cavern's throat whose darkness shook
To the engulphéd murmur of a stream,
Snoring within his dusky mountain lair.
And the less fearless twain made light of him
Who rashly struck with bold spear unreversed
The shield of Peril, toying with his life.
They goaded him with barbs of dextrous wit,
Pelted his brows with showers of dainty spleen,

But he nor moved nor smiled, but prone on earth
Listened as though he heard them not, then said :

" I saw pale Helen wander lonely-eyed,
Unsceptred of her beauty ; saw the stare
Of cold Medusa when she sat apart ;
I saw Ixion wrestle with his wheel,
And Tityus smite the vulture ; and I danced
In lampless halls with young Eurydice,
Chatted with Ceres' daughter and took lunch
With Pluto.   Would you hear the song he sang ? "
And lifting up a treble voice he sang.

> Let Jove rub bright his milky-way,
>   And brother Neptune scour his floor,
> I 'll hold my wassail night and day,
>   And hear my sea of sinners roar.
> I choose before celestial ruffles
>   My easy suit of Stygian grey.

> You 're just from the Academy?
>   I love your snowy saintships there ;
> Though they blaspheme me shamefully,
>   I 've filled each professorial chair,
> And when they rally for devotion,
>   They sometimes let me make a prayer.

> But mostly ye are fools and shrimps
>   To put the devil under ban.
> As theologue he slightly limps,
>   I grant, but he 's a gentleman ;

His vaults are packed with earth's best vintage ;
    Proserpina, fill up the can.

He was a sprightly German thrush
    Who sang my tail off, stole my gear,
And left me breeches, frills and plush.
    I love the Teutons at their beer,
But when they 're transcendentalistic, —
    God bless me, but I 'd rather hear

Jove's stamp of wrath that shocks the pole,
    Or Corybantes when at wine,
Than their accursed prophets roll
    Voluminous periods half-divine.
A secret, sir, — to exorcise me
    Make the idealistic sign.

One last full beaker, — is it warm ?
    Just bear my compliments, I pray,
Up to your friends.   I mean no harm.
    But should they chance to lose their way,
Be sure I 'd do the hospitable.
    My blessing with you, sir, good day.

The twain laughed loud, and the grave Master smiled.
But when these frolic matin moods had ebbed,
They sought the landscape that was hung serene
Before them, a Hesperian scope that clomb
Northward from champaign unto champaign fair,
In slow ascension, till the silver haze
Languished in dreamy distance ; pastoral types

Of lovely contour, melting line in line,
Bold angles, winding mazes, gentle curves,
Mild slopes, basked in the rich dividuous Light,
Thereon unfolding all her tissues bright,
Cashmeres and damasks, lustrous tyrians,
Orange and auburn and deep lazuli.
And over all were sown with happy art
The cultured spaces, orchat valleys, groves,
Green pastures, sinuous silvers, sheets of glass,
White farmsteads, gleaming steeples, smiling vills ;
And, intercepted by the jealous cliff,
Higher, the luminous fragment of a lake,
Suspended like a crescent ; and beyond,
The limit and blue-breasted shore of all,
A ridge of mountain propping skies that sank
From weight of their own splendor ; azure fields,
Wherein the thronging fleeces in full flock
Pastured at leisure, mimicked underneath
By loitering shadows browsing up the hills.
And these who nursed acquaintance with the lore
Artistic, conned the features of the scene
In liquid pedantries, caught up at school,
Of tint and mezzotint, chiaroscuro,
Thence touched upon the neighboring world of books,
Mixing with sensuous sweets abstruse delights
Of critic and discussive thought, until
With high and philosophic parle profound,
They sweetly countercharmed all sylvan sights,
Rapt on the inner motions of the mind.

But Vivian, long time mute because their words,

Though lined with classic graces, edged with wit
That smote the critic spark from every theme,
Fell on his troubled soul like flakes of fire,
Said bitterly, " I too once plied with joy
The loom of speech ornate, was proud to spin
My gossamer so fine it would afford
No footing to a sunbeam, or to tilt,
Empanoplied in logic and the like,
With trenchant swoops of burnished subtleties ;
Fondest to lead the struggling topic bound
With links ratiocinative ; but no more.
For whom the great gulfs swallow, marshals not
His agony in sleek euphonious phrase.
I move through flaming deserts overswept
By thirsty winds, smothered by sandy drifts ;
And battered on the pebbly hills or tossed
On arid tides, languish afar from aid,
Weak fledgling of a zone of temperate skies ;
Or like the sea-god of untoward fate,
Float on the brine forlorn by headlands hoar,
The brother of the monster and the storm,
Weak, weary, maimed, forever bruised and torn,
Wearing upon my breast and thighs the stains,
The dross and cockle of a thousand shores."

And Arthur answered, half compassionate,
" Sad-hearted, ever piping mournful strains,
Compact of riddling, melancholy hints,
Wherefore pronounce so darkly of this ill
That would usurp your mind ?   Perchance 't is but
A phantom, that if broached with hardy words

Or orbed about with clearer light, will pass.
The thought, turned burning to explore within,
Teems with illusion.   Wiser who pursues
Expanse of vision, more embracing scope,
A larger circle.   I am irked to see
Eyes always downcast, this despondent brow,
These lone and sombre broodings without smile,
In you whom all aforetime wont to praise
A bubbling fount of jocund fellowship,
A lavish sower of congenial talk,
Flying the light and laughter-trailing jest.
I hoped these peaks would lose your gathering clouds
Of heaviness in sounding showers of joy.
O why sit palsied, moaning to the past,
Ah darlings days, forever lost to me,
When will the period of the years present
Once more your features !   'T is a better lore
That from courageous hearts the Infinite
Is never distant, proffering her wealth."

And Vivian smiled a little as he said,
His accent lightly tipped with irony,
" O rare condoler, whose smooth pity soothes
Gentlier than softest oil these biting wounds !
O happy friend, to whose enfranchised eye
The great world shows a crystal bead of dew,
From film to film transpicuous !   You err,
Hoping with remedies so light and swift
To charm from these fierce pangs their bitterness.
I ask not of the past her jovial quips,
Hollow and vain in this oppressive hour.

Nor needs it that you set your words with thorns,
And tender tauntings of a mind too weak,
Or drag in valor like a bold magician,
Whose arts will exorcise the soul's despair.
Can valor hang the inky firmament
With starry lamps, or launch the sun on high,
Or bid the darkling moon renew her smiles?
'T is light, sweet light of heaven's own christening,
Fresh from the unfathomable eyes of God,
For whose transcendent loveliness I yearn.
But man beats up a darkness with his light,
And this the rigorous thought would purge away,
Though eye and cheek be widowed of their lustres,
And the proud form be wasted to a shred."

Then Arthur, "Little of these doubts I know.
Not angling with the dialectic bait,
Nor spreading cunning toils of argument
May we make captive the deft element,
The mystic soul of life, our sum of truth.
What profit these ingenious sophistries,
Light jugglery of narrow intellects,
The glitter and the pride of peacock wits!
The bird of boldest wing, most fearless eye,
Trails not these gaudy hindrances.   There are,
Who follow truth as sportsmen chase the hart,
Loving the sparkling joyance of pursuit,
The unleashed ardors of the quickened blood,
More than her proper being.   These will loose
The balanced shaft or poise the javelin
To make revealment of their supple thews,

Leaving the game to moulder. I love not
The metaphysic and inquisitive
Dividing eye, rich in refining arts,
Disdainful of the living hand. O square
Your purposes to the advancing time,
And mingle with her labors. The first stroke
Will sweep your heavens, like a thunder-besom,
Bare of these gathering vapors."
                And his words,
In earnestness so pitched above their wont,
Drew smiles from Paul and Vivian. Vivian then,
"O friend, whose thought is clear as summer pools,
I wronged you, deeming that your sympathy
Slighted my hour of trial as the wan
And sickly fancy of a straining mind,
That dealt with its own shadows, or would pluck
At visionary baubles. But this bold
Disclosure of a sure redeeming aid
Hits not the front of my necessity.
Labor long-plied amid the fervid crowd
May dull the promptings of the heart's desire,
As fools may drown disaster in their wine.
But this large hope that leads me on, foot-charmed,
Grows but by clearness of the eye within.
Until the higher cycle fill its flower,
I cannot pause to mould the things of sense.
For ah, not thus the speculative mind
May be defrauded of his ample realm,
And that imperial sceptre which he bears.
His irreversible great period
He must fulfil, though baffled by the folds

Of a beguiling darkness ; and not less
Burgeons a faith that some bright light will fall
From heaven upon me and complete my hope.
But now the night oppresses.   Feeling round
With hands of inquiry, I oft alight
On monsters of the midnight.   Demons flock,
And spectres startle.   Mocked by every wind,
The spirit aspirant to holiness
Pours all his golden homage at the feet
Of gods that perish.   Gorgonizing eyes
Stare on me from the wide and visible world.
Turning the lenses inward, I am awed
By fearful mysteries whose dusky wings
Shadow the wondrous thing we name the Self,
And all it can and cannot, may not, may ;
And by those giant-browed antagonisms,
Whose marriage must prelude the birth of life.
Yea, and my soul is tenfold more confused
By glimpses of the god-like Ultimate
That glows in gold on peaks of the Ideal,
Beheld at times from these thick-misted vales,
Wherein I falter.   Over all, the spell,
The monstrous shadow of a creed that took
Prisoner the boyish heart in its first prayers,
Broods and confounds.   I am infirm to pass
And thrid the gordian glooms of unbelief."

Then Paul, the dreaming elf, who would have loved
Of old to haunt the Mercotic wave
With anchoretic fancies ; he who urged
The lower duties languidly, though tuned

Most finely unto high idealisms,
Broke out in ringing accents, silver-clear,
Raised from their wonted soft Eolian flow;
"You spake of the Ideäl. Can the voice,
Once freighted with the sweetness of this note,
Relapse to sounds of sorrow? Lo, it stands
Afar, the perfect circle which the ages move
To finish, or the perfect melody
Whose strong sweet thunders aye enchant the ears
Of high-enthroned eternity, or yet
The perfect poem, epos of all time,
God's art. And most men make a word, but some
A line, and some with souls of heavenly fire
A rhythmic sentence, words and sense complete.
Behold the lordly solace of all ills,
The Ideäl, if we follow it with love,
Not fainting; and its radiance is the sure
Sole revelation of our God Most High.
O then pursue it through all wrongs of time.
Onward, through gloom of mist and dash of hail,
Onward, through bolts of scorn and mockery,
Onward, through life and death until there dawn
The greater life and bathe the soul in light."

And from the depths of his despondency,
The mournful voice of Vivian slowly came.
"O Paul, you bear an ardent prophet-heart,
By nature lifted o'er this troubled sphere,
To catch the brightness of a statelier morn
To which our mortal prime is patched and wan;
Fortunate too, in those who early shaped

The plastic spirit.   For these glowing words
I needs must love you.   But you aim amiss.
Shooting sublime above my head you skip
My lowly plight.   For yet between us roars
A gulf which not my boldest faith can bridge,
Abysmal, drear.   I mark the rosy hopes,
The pride and inspiration of my youth,
Turn pale and fall, transpierced with shafts of death,
The strong colossal purposes, like snow,
Thaw to a gliding wave.   This doubt has grown
In fierce Satanic hardihood, and laid
His giant arms about the seated plinths
Of nature and wellnigh has tugged away
The firm and old foundations of the world.
The day may come, perchance the morn will break,
When I shall mount on some celestial wing,
And catch these splendors where they have their
        birth."

Perceiving that his time of passion wore
His heart, the white-haired Father said, with looks
Kindled by love and earnest sympathy,
" My son, your keel must ride tempestuous seas.
But lose not hope.   Days dutiful to truth,
Though subject long to tempest, are secure.
Endure and wrestle and the end will come.
The fashions of the world are manifold,
But the divine eternity is one.
There are to whom the burthen of the age
Is grievous, and its work and worship seem
Maimed of their lawful beauty.   These must sail

From sheltered harbors past the promontories,
Into the boundless ocean.   And of these,
My son, are you.   Fear not, for you will reach
Fortunate isles, and margins paved with gold,
Beauteous abodes, the haunts of dewy peace,
Winds musical and low.   O lose not hope.
Ever the noble mind when transient
From certain to uncertain, old to new,
Must plant a passing foot on skepticism.
Doubt guards with dragon-coil the sweet demesne,
Where truth, belief and worship grow, and hang
Three golden apples, the Hesperian fruit
Of life, whose winning is the end of man.
If this be conquered, lo, a land is yours
Where hang the ripest blossoms of the world,
Where, cherished on the sweets of rich repose,
The soul, 'gainst all degrees of tainting clay,
Itself shall temper to heroic use."

Then Arthur cried for luncheon, from his throat
To chase Plutonian savors, as he said.
So they brake fast, and where a gurgling rill
Mantled his shelvy coves with drifts of spume,
Appeased their thirst.   "The cavern there," said
        Paul,
" Has breathed upon us with Trophonian gloom,
A power of sadness.   Rise, let us forego
Threnetic notes, and slip to yon fair world,
Whose bright eye haunts me with a sense of bliss ;
And as the prelude to a livelier strain,
I 'll sound a welcome to the spirit of Joy,

Our guide and chosen compeer till the eve."
And while they moved across the vale, he sang:

He stands on the mountains,
　　He darts through the vallies,
From the foam of the fountains
　　He laughs and he sallies,
He leaps in the torrent, he speaks in the thunder,
　　Gaily flashing and flowing,
　　　　His fire and his passion
　　Lead him on, ever growing
　　　　Diviner in fashion,
Arrayed in fresh hues and new garments of wonder.

　　　Has he a palace?
　　　　Where is his ærie?
　　　　With spirits of faery
　　　He haunts the sweet chalice
　　　　Of lily or rose ;
　　Or clothed with the glances,
　　　　The soft crimson glows
　　From cool eyes of morning,
　　　　He weaves his wild dances
　　Of laughter and scorning,
　Through far cerulean fields ;
　　　　Or rides a strong warrior
　　　　Over rock, moat, and barrier,
　　To pierce the heart of darkness
　With the million darts he wields ;
　　　　Or thrids a bright maiden
　　　　The tangles of our dreams,

To awaken and gladden
  With auroral smiles and beams.
This is the bearer
  Of music and mirth,
The broad world shows fairer
  In manhood and worth,
When his light pinions sound up the meadows,
To perch in our household shadows.
  The secret and subtle
  Swift dance of life's shuttle
    Obeys his desire.
  On the day's mighty bosom
  The hours burst in blossom
    Of heavenly fragrance and fire.
  Comes a presence of beauty
    To soothe and caress us,
  A strength for all duty
    To lift and to bless us,
  And the yoke of endeavor
  Sits light as a flower,
  While our souls grow forever
  In sweetness and power.
O, elf-king, we love thee, thy heart is so glad,
Come with us, that we too may forget to be sad.

They traced a meagre path that crawled in fear
The giddy margin of the dark abyss,
Naked, save where a lonely bush, depth-charmed,
Leaned out with all its buds against the void,
Like some fair maid that ends a fierce despair;
Young Sappho toppling from the island crag.

Thence through a rocky breadth of woodland old
Descending, they espied not far a slope
Rippling with arid shoals of tawny wheat,
That fought with rock and sun for a lean ear,
Flung like a foam-wreath from the surging sea
Of tillage.　But anon they met a breath
Of meadowy balm, and in a pastured glade
Touched foot on sward and found the cots of men.
Pausing a space within a cool recess,
What time the aged sire regained his breath,
They watched a merle, his dainty cowl back thrown,
Cloistered in leaves, confess his nut-brown mate,
Keeping a hard suspicion in his eye ;
But as she closed, he trilled an allegro,
A rich, absolving note.　Listening they heard
The copse-clad shoulder of the woodland heave
And palpitate, and looking, saw not far
A form whose broad and battlemented breast
Clove the full leafage as a swimmer cleaves
A sleeping water, till upon them fell
His booming stride of thunder.　And they turned
To fix a curious stare on eyes, whose glance,
Couched under beetling shagginess, leaped forth
From deeps of autumn gray, a force to seize
And tear piecemeal the thing whereon it fell.
Ten paces off he halted.　And what time
The green wake of his coming slept again,
And ebbed the echoes of his footing, shod
With clangor, firm he stood, columnar, calm,
Striking on all their forms with whetted looks,
Coursing from forehead unto foot, again

With critic leisure upward, till he met
The smile that rippled o'er the cheek of Paul,
Offering salute.   Half grimly then he said,
"A stranger in these parts, I take it, sir."
And Paul, "You have not missed.   We sought a land
Fattest in kine and milk and cheese, and here
We find it Canaan wheresoe'er we move.
A courteous friend has made us happy guests,
And teaches us the marvels of the land."

And glancing on the Sire, the farmer said,
"Methinks this is the man whom people call
The fool of maniac fancies, airy-brained,
Long locked within a rugged mountain glen.
Some name him infidel and atheist,
Mystic, philosopher, and pantheist,
Or transcendent—, God help my barn-yard wit,
I cannot drag their chain of syllables.
Some say, his words have little meaning in them,
And some, though there, 't is hard to come across.
But I, a settler here these latter years,
Know nought of him, save what the ear has picked
From random rumors.   Yet my heart loves not
Monastic pratings in these rotten days,
When states are piloted by false pretense,
And low intrigue usurps the seats of rule.
God strike the feeble leaders of the times
With hermit fancies.   But for every man,
Let him come down into the world and aid
His narrow brethren of the bounded earth."

Such words and more to his impassioned thought
Gave vent tempestuous, while either arm
Was wheeled in fiery circle.   When his tides
Had dashed themselves to foam, the three brake out
In laughter loud, prolonged and reboant,
That frightened every echo.   But again
He flashed in monstrous wit, with rolling eyes
Fresh-frenzied from his soul.
                    " And who are ye
That play so liberal with your mirth?   Ye seem
Some of that pale-cheeked swarm of aping wits,
Who from their pedant desks buzz round our farms,
Profound with sage, outlandish theories
And slothful doctrine, teaching, men should rust
Eremite, banished from industrious ways,
Battening on vacant thoughts of God knows what,
With scorn of common strivings.   College-boys,
Bantlings of thin chameleon diet, their
Small brains awry from meddling with the books,
Or packed with speculative stuff that seems
True knowledge, come with shrill grasshopper chirp,
High-browed contempt and academic strut,
To turn adrift the wisdom of their sires,
And smile away their modes.   With hands of silk
And sinews sapless grown from arid ease,
They hope to choke the monsters of the world,
And blunt the thorns of life.   Not theirs the force
To grapple with the labor and the pain,
With sufferance and persistence to unlock
The oracular lips of living wisdom.   Bah!
These are a little folk, the spawn of the time."

Again they laughed.   But Paul ceased first and said,
" Amid the weltering currents of these days
All keels of worth anchor in secret calm,
And seek the covert arms of windless coves.
I doubt not there are men of rural thoughts,
Names not yet bandied by the crowd, whose hands
Could harness this wild turbulence to wheels
Of nobler triumphs than we know, or hold
The helm of ordinance firmly to the Just.
These souls, if you could lure them from their nooks,
Might purge the civic ministration, build
A people strong and noble, through defects
Of fear or surging shocks of circumstance,
Advance their kingly purposes, and found
More during nationality."
                    But then
Arthur let loose his wonted fierce disdain :
" Miraculous statesmen these !   Rare kings of men!
Fie, Paul, you lack acquaintance with the world.
Your eyes droop alway, and you miss the thing
That woos you to observe it.   Who would ride
The storm, must like the eagle first make strong
His wings by buffeting its thunder-breath.
Ha, ha, God help your sceptred anchorites.
Far wiser they to tend their cabbages,
To train the rose or list the robin pipe,
Than feed the popular dragon on the cates
Of delicate idealisms.   Behold,
On all sides jars of bias and degree,
A blatant discord hoarse and bold, would fright
Their soft ears sensitive to woodland notes,

Or stealthy springes of fine policy
Trip them from magisterial heights.   O kings !"

And while he spake, the farmer's wrath was laid,
As angry feathers on a falcon's neck
Sink one by one.   From point to point they passed,
Until the frozen sweetness of his soul
Thawed to a kindly flow of courtesy,
Deep, musical.   And pointing out his grange,
He urged them to make trial of his board,
His garden-fruits, his cider and his beef,
And see the wonders of his farm.   They went.
And then his mellow tones of welcome fell
As ripe as russets from the boughs of autumn.
Forsaking wood and dell, they crossed a mead
That drank his footsteps, caught anon the house,
Trim as a lass that waits her lover, flanked
By ample lengths of storehouse and of barn.
And from the porch shot, like a stream of light,
Or foamy cataract dipping in the dusk
Of hanging rocks, Margaret, the farmer's child.
On light and fairy-twinkling feet she came
In maiden glee, her rubious lips apart
With treble welcome.   But, the strangers spied,
Her graceful motions fluttered into rest,
Like doves that float to earth, their buoyant wings
Shot-crippled on a sudden.   So she hung
In sweet dismay, until the father's lips,
Closing on hers, restored her.   And they passed
To the inner cool, and gladly, hunger-bit,
Found spread the table, and the cider drawn.

They dined. The cider circled. The discourse
Sparkled with many a lustre, like a brook,
Wayward; laughing from trivial theme to theme
With vagrant impulse, slowly deepening down
To one full flood of wisdom from the host
On that which made the perfect farmer, how
The flocks are fitliest handled, how the crops,
The times, the seasons, economic laws
That dealing out full measure, dealt not out
To poorness and perpetual emptiness.
His speech, aflame with native idiom,
Keen-phrased and topic-cleaving like a spear,
Dashed them in torrent. And then Arthur said,
" My fortune, sir, to-day has half begot
Resolve to quit the haunts of learned brows,
Put by the hopes that pointed to the heights
Of place and fame, and couched in rustic peace,
Wed wisdom to repose, and glean by love
Lessons of beauty from all simple things.
Those rare and golden moods wherefrom are born
The thoughts which are a music in themselves,
And murmur round the lips of lofty men,
Are wooed and won by these sweet-breathing days,
That enter sandaled with soft silence, stoled
In robes of household quietness, with gifts
Of mellow leisure, tempered by all sights
And sounds the meadows offer and the groves."

The farmer answered him with words that twanged
Like strings just lightened of the shaft. " Not you.
I read a better story in your eye.

Your soul is strained to action, and to hold
In poise the lightnings of the State, to feel
The vital pulses of all purposes.
I love you better for it.   Give me breath.
I bustle or I die.   But who would drone
Forever in the hive, when all around
Are tasked with noble functions?   Bah! the heart
Is sickened.   And I think the race of men
Grows feebler down from sire to son; more greed,
Less sufferance ; and God knows the end.
Books may be well to help a sleepy hour
When rains are on the roof, or monstrous snows
Have penned us in the fold.   But son of mine
Shall never thin his brain with watery stuff
That idle poets brew, nor snarl his thoughts
With knots and tangles which our pigmy wits
Tie and untie, and name philosophy."
But when his weaponed glances, roving round,
Came to the full-orbed wonder in the eyes
Of Margaret, love disarmed them.   And he said,
" Nay, sweet one, this is true.   And heed you well
That when the seasons have full-blown the rose
It lavish not its heart on every breeze
That wantons round its petals.   Yea, I swear
You shall not taste of wifehood, but shall pass
The years in maiden ponderings, ere you wed
A delicate cavalier of this plume,
Who, all serene in musk and oil and glove,
Rides to convince the world of judgment.   Bah!
I 'd yoke these essenced suitors to the plough,
And bruise their snowy palms with axe and spade,

Forcing them toil, like Jacob, many years
For her they loved."
        And Margaret blushed and laughed.
But Paul, who could but think this bolt, though
    aimed
Askance, was loosed to glance on him, laughed loud.
They rose and moved to spy the mammoth farm,
Fallow, and tilth, and pasture. Past them danced
The maiden Margaret, hasting blithe afield,
Bearing a well-stored basket, to refresh
The fainting hearts of the worn laborers.
About her sang the fragrant meadow airs,
And with her went a gladness and a grace,
One with the sweet breath of the swarming flowers,
And the besieging noise of golden bees,
And far before, a force, of her approach
Prelude, that touched the toilers in the maize
With stillness, and their gazing eyes with love.
Then one led up a ruddy cow, dark-hoofed ;
" A four-year-old in March," the farmer said,
" My dairy-queen, I had her brought for you.
She takes the prize next autumn." And he conned
Her alphabet of beauty slowly o'er :
Long face, clear jaw, fineness of curving horn,
Full chine and heavy flank and breadth of loin,
Bold eyes and clear, which all the herd obey,
Straight back, wide hips, neat shoulder, slender
    thigh,
Thin tail and glossy hair, as soft as silk.
And when she moved, he bade them mark her gait,
Free motions, supple joints, and stately port.

He named his duties, spread them out through
    lengths
Of critic dissertation ; to his plans
The measure of fulfillment granted, or
How finely framed and aptly into act
Translated ; sowing here and there the hints
Of a conceiving, keen supremacy ;
Last, showed a long-nursed hope that in his heart
Smouldered like Etna on from year to year,
Yet unessayed, but biding there its hour,
Spoke of its reason, manner, scope, and growth,
And large prosperities that would attend
Its consummation.   Radiant then from all,
His full disclosure, their rapt audience —
The transient spleen that clouded his first looks
Flung down in tempest — forth from eye and cheek
The latent sun of kindness brake in splendor.
The afternoon slipped past them like a ghost,
Till with the level sun was slowly said
Farewell, followed by lingering words, again
Farewell, the while he crushed their pulpy palms
In one that might have rent the lion, bronzed
From unreluctant toil.   In genial mood
Homeward, as the first dews came down, they strolled.

In front the sunset waned ; a glorious arch,
Whereon the seas of beauty brake in foam
Of gold ; grandeur not overgrand, but mild
And perceant through meekness.   And behind,
Grey twilight built the pillars of her home.
Above, through argent-rippling tides the moon,

Sweet-gliding argosy of poets' joys,
Drove her translucent beak through firth and strait.
They strode into the west with souls that drank
The triple heaven, lips mute and asking eyes,
Until there fell a darkness and they all
Breathed freer, found again themselves and talked.
Child of the evening, beautiful, serene,
The Patriarch held them thralled with ripest words,
Named in that sacred hour all mystic names,
Wove symbols, builded types, unfolded laws;
Shattered a drop of truth to radiant spray,
Ravished the fragrant heart of flowering thought
With a sciential witchery as of heaven,
Or edified with plastic force remote
Conceptions, till they stood instinct with form;
Upon the tremulous spaces of the night
Loosing melodious rivers, until each
Knew surely that it was the golden Age.

III.

BRUISED with travail, dark in mind,
Stung from land to land in vain,
Yearns the harried youth to find
Oasis to cool his brain,
To stay awhile his flaming quest
And lull the clamor in his breast.

Gentle goddess of the sphere,
Nature hears his piteous wail,
Plies her facile hands to rear,
Heart-deep in umbrageous vale,
Opiate bowers whose poppied pillows
Lure delicious sleep to furl
Wings of languor. Crystals curl
Round its woof in whispering billows,
Soothest, drowsiest in their purl.

From her pipe gush sweeter strains
Than the pathos of Apollo
When the passion thrilled his veins
By Daphne in Thessalian hollow.
The youth forgets his mortal pains,
Charmed in will, he hastes to follow :
Odorous glooms and alleys thrids,

Sinks in her luxurious blisses,
While she presses honied kisses
On his slow-unwrinkled lids ;
Summons bees from violet dells
To steal the melrose from its cells
And feed his slumber-budded lips.
From yellow skirts of pendulous bells,
Meadowy awns, or scented drips
Pimpling the lily's glowing eaves,
Cicadas pluck the fresh-orbed dew
To cool his temples through and through.
O'er his roseate thighs she snows
Crocus, pansy, dark primrose ;
Softer croons than wooing turtle
Spells that deepen his repose ;
Wand of amber cinct with myrtle
Waves, and through her dusk pavilion
Sails young Phantasy on pinions
Golden, purple and vermilion,
While the ambrosial shadows tingle,
Where his train of burnished minions,
Dreams and visions, flit and mingle.
These shall pilot his calm sleep
Through balmy twilights slumber-deep,
And make in baths of mildest splendor
His spirit white and moist and tender.

She will keep thee, darling child,
Young and whole and undefiled.
For she caught thee and first brought thee
From the far celestial forges,

Where from inorganic night,
Glowing with immortal light,
The young soul of man emerges.
In these fragrant robes she wraps thee,
In these golden visions laps thee,
In the silence of thy blossom.
And her love for thee is deeper
Than all seas and skies, sweet sleeper.
Shielded in her inmost bosom,
Thou shalt hear the mystic beating,
Thine shall be the awful greeting.

———◆———

" No jarring mood to-day, nor fretful thought.
Fold up the sombre weeds of gloom and take
The garments of the morning.   Flush the heart
With light, and fill the waking eyes with joy.
Come up, appareled in the grace of youth,
Into auroral gardens, and in bowers
Of sunrise and of sunset and the blue
Pavilions pitched by the meridian day,
From brimming beakers all his lyric hours
Quaff nectar, which a hundred Hebes bring ;
The gush, the gleam, the fragrance and the bloom,
Assiduous murmurs, floating minstrelsies,
Cerulean tints, the orange glow, the rose,
Earth, air and sky in triple ecstasy.
Come forth, and we will move until we find
Altars of nature fitly garlanded,

There to lay down our gifts of reverence.
For who will dare to mock these shining hours
With eyes that fetch their light from suns long set,
Or hopes that are not born from them, but chafe
The heart to a warm foam ! But we will rove
Chasing a bird's wing, and will lose our way
With every arch misleading brook that calls.
These lightly-spun vagaries will beguile
Dark fancies, and with souls that can obey
The sweet impulsions of a later hour,
The sober warnings and high questionings,
Will we return when all the murmuring vans
Forsake the shutting portals of the flower,
And this slow semi-circle round the pine,
Travelled by his own shade, is drawn full curve."

So to his young initiate the Sire,
Just as in dewy dusks of breathless boughs,
The flutes, long time to finest warblings tuned,
Chimed into full orchestral prologue clear,
Greeting that greater bird whose mighty breast,
Fire-flushed through all its down, now slowly rose
From eyries hung upon his orient cliffs.
And when the motions of his wings made heave
The air with breezy billows, they slipped down
Into the blossomed levels of the world
Among the mellow-throated kine and heard
The early cow-boy peal his loud halloo,
The cock fife shrilly and the peacock scream
Across the gathering murmur of the land.
Full summer throbbed in the pulse of things and lent

The bough its densest umbrage, on the wing,
That flitted, seemed to shed its fairest hues,
Mellowed the streams and with a balanced palm
Began to round the apple and to turn
Upon her lathe the neck of the young pear.
She spun again the frequent rose, relaced
The slender bodice of the lily, sowed
The willing daisy in all meads, and fanned
The thickets into tongues of flowery fire ;
Into the cherry's orbing cheek imbreathed
Its various lustre and unto the peach
The silken earnest of its ripeness, gave.
Most fearless nestled in her lap the lark,
Embowering a covert for her young,
And in green grots on his depending cells
Wrought the unresting bee, thoughtless of harm.
Thus she, a glowing vintage, helped the brain
Of the creative year to body forth
His music and his passion into forms
Of visible life.
                    With lingering steps they moved.
And where the dairies, packed in mottled herd,
Urged patiently the never wearied jaw,
They caught the glint of furbished cans that
          brimmed
With creamy foam, and, plump in arm and waist,
Their foreheads buried in the silky flank,
The milk-maids pressing fulsome udders down.
The turkey-cock let fall his glossy fans
And marched in strut before them ; in the grass,
Filled with maternal fears the clucking hen

Stalked midmost of her brood of chirping chicks,
With eye and beak that hunted worm and midge.
On cribs half plundered of their golden store
The pigeon pruned her purples, or soft cooed
From roof to roof. They heard the fervid hives,
Under the broad limbs of ancestral elms,
Hum up and down their snowy lines with swarms
Of rival peoples going in and out,
Serfs, kings and queens and thronged ambassadors,
Thigh-laden with the tribute of the fields.
In garden plots the timely matron purged
Her beds of weed insidious, while yet
The soil, dew-tender, gave her leave. And lo,
Majestic with complacent footsteps slow,
Through every province of his fat estate,
His geese, his ducks, his horses and his kine,
Moved forth and back the arbiter of all,
The mammoth landlord, bellied like a whale,
Cloud-crowned with incense rendered to himself
From carven censer of a monstrous pipe.
All round were breadths of wheat in saffron glow,
Full-ripe and bending down a teeming ear
Meekly, while banded reapers struck in tune,
And formed the equal swath. In clovery crofts
Echoed the clinking cog where stealthy blades,
Darting like light their keen and glittering fangs
Within dark sheaths, shore from the dimpled cheeks
Of all the rosy knolls the virgin beard.
In half-cropt pastures fled the wanton colt,
Or shook his unkempt mane across the rails,
Contemplative with curious eye and ear.

And dusky quires that peopled every holt
Struck loud the choric cymbal, without jar,
And alway in a mesh of his own strains
Tangled, the bobolink fluttered overhead.

Drunk with the ambrosial liquor which the day
Had pressed since early morn against their lips,
Weary of voyaging the billowy beams,
Upon a lawny isle of thickest shade
Stranded, they lay, and drowsed to languorous
        dreams,
What time in cloudless zenith flamed the sun.
This was a scented cool of lofty woods,
Furrowed with dingles, starred with rose-thickets,
Slope-fledge with hazel. Upon clustering banks
Couched round in genial mood at ample ease,
They drank a wind that, sighing from the south,
Embraced the amorous aspen and enforced
Quick tones of love and pressed with fragrant lips,
Fresh from amours with all the meadow flowers,
Delightful kisses on their brows. In front,
Smooth as a sea becalmed from shore to shore,
The champaign stretched his lazy length afar ;
Broad leas, luxuriant woodlands, shining creeks,
The waving maize, the yellow grain, the math,
And eastward the great lake in silver sheen,
Sown with white flakes of sail. The hills were lapt
In fire and breezes tipped their plumes with flame.
The browsing kine forsook the sunny wolds,
Huddled in leafy twilights of the brakes,
Closing their eyes and by their odorous breath

Alluring humming swarms of parasites.
The brindled ox before his burden trailed
Reluctantly the alternating hoof,
And lagging teamsters spared the leathern thong.
The couchant lark was hid in grassy nooks,
Nor cooed the wild dove from his firry bough.
But in the sultry surf that chafed their strand,
To shivery pipes in morrice wild the thin
Cicada danced and solemn butterflies
Floated on dappled wings, and sweetly gleamed
The girdles of a hundred hasting bees,
Or at long spells a vagrant humming-bird
Fanned cool a fainting rose with restless plumes.
Only were heard chewink, pewee or wren,
Or nut-hatch beating lonely drum, or tit
Sounding his lullaby.   Great Pan unfurled
His sluggish lids and from his hairy lips
Down dropped the morning pipe whose warbled joy,
Bubbling from million stops, had wearied all
The echoes, sweet as when he charmed his founts
Mænalian or his groves in Homole.
Great Pan grew faint and loosed his shagginess
Where woodland shuttles wove a seamless shade,
In dreamy ambush stretched, while downy airs
Breathed lethe, and the world was hush to nurse
His slumber into full oblivious depths.

From dozy noddings waked, they mused a space
Silent, till Paul flung out a passionate strophe ;
" Not Araby nor Arcady, all sweet
Castalian sounds, nor choicest scents of Ind

Vie with thy wondrous round of blandishments
Nor match the myriad charms that meet in thee,
O pride of summer days, whose golden feet
Sport on the blue slopes of a thousand hills,
Whose wings with soft ambrosial murmurings
Distill creative heat into thy heart,
O world !   Even that proud forsaken one
Of Florence, loneliest, mournfullest, his eyes
Soothed from their fiery wanderings on thy face,
His passion calmed from that supremest heaven,
Had owned no fairer sight in Paradise."

And Vivian then in passionate antistrophe,
" Ah me, to be a child, a simple child
Of nature, couched within her lap and thrilled
With warm and rhythmic pulses of delight
From her dear hand, to watch her stately eyes
Yearning from clear deeps of maternal joy,
To drink melodious utterance of her love
Steeping the bruised soul in happy tears,
To catch the burning oracles that well
Fresh-fountained from her lips with gentle ease
Past Delphic, while mild valor would conform
The rounded scope and purpose of the soul
Unto the holy rigor of her law !"

"O well, in sooth, my son," the Master said.
" Forever far from you the hollow speech,
The light lip-wooings, fickle janty loves,
Mock adorations of lean hearts who sound
Her lofty titles on unholy lips,

And chant about her lightning-girdled throne
The profanation of obsequious praise :
For whom she keeps disdain, eternal, cold.
Far, too, the paltry arrogance of crude
Unloving souls, who would from God divorce
His chosen forms, divest him of his worlds,
In which he is appareled from of old.
Nor these she pities, but from her sublime
Abysses hurls derision loud and deep.
She would be viewed with meekest poet-eyes,
And to the imperious knock of worldly men
Frames her response in meagre syllables.
Is nature stark? And wear her lips no smile?
And do her plastic hands nothing create ?
Behold, she breathes, she moves, and forward bears
Time and the spaces and the stars with her.
Yea, man, this creature of divinest pangs,
Prone child of prayers and upward-yearning eyes,
Upon her voyages the vast Inform
Unto a shore for which he ever peers
And sees not. Most unsearchably she holds
Her marble robes about her awful face,
Nor can we speak of that eternal goal
She goes to touch, but through her sacred veil
Love radiates, and glimpses of the Good.
Nor deem it lightly uttered here, that one,
Who from his cradle has gone forth with her,
The glad and childlike mirror of her moods,
Sharing her sorrows and her joys, has roamed
Disconsolate amid her dark eclipse,
And dazed his soul against her splendor-brows,

And on the billows of her effluent smile
Played like a sea-god, boldly should pronounce
That what he best has known or deepest felt,
Love, passion, worship or clear ecstasy,
Has had in her its day-spring and from her
Has blessed him and uplifted.   'T is ordained
That thus the soul of man should be evoked,
And made a reverent witness of itself.
From the full fountain of the heart go forth
Sweet influences of delight that teach
The wide and dark abysses to be fair.
And that within beholds itself without,
Mirrored in the transpicuous universe,
And thus beholding, knows itself divine.
For what the cloud withholds the star reveals,
And what I find not in the silver sea
Sleeping all day upon his sunny shores,
The rich and glossy folds of the great Deep
Beyond the stars, rain softly down on me.
And thus all forms and motions of the world
Lure forth the soul to know herself and find
Her limits vanishing like mists of dawn,
Her sphere containing and uniting all,
Her paths slow-widening to the infinite.
This is her heavenly dower of liberty,
Her dearest gift, a beauty not her own.
Yet know, my children, ever since the mind
Contemplative has poured a light full-orbed,
Great hearts have leaned unto the godly faith,—
Unproven, should it chance, thereby a faith
The more insensuous, whose hands reach out

Past dialectic and the thought's concept,—
That nature from her rising to her set,
Her lordly elements, her ordinance,
Streams forth in mystic effluence from the soul,
Not brute nor diverse ; a white beam unseen,
But on the bosom of an evening cloud
Impinged, a spray of colors ; or a sea
That breaks his steadfast calm from zone to zone
To joy in his own beauty and to catch
The shimmer of his countless crests.   Thus she,
From the one soul inseparate, to man
Is symbol of that more majestic man
He marches to become ; a hope, a zeal,
A piety.   Thus she in him, but he
In fulness of the imperishable soul,
Finds his due term.   In her as in a rose
God blossoms into beauty for a day,
From her as from a solemn organ draws
The melodies of being, blowing out
Through all her reeds the indivisible life.
For as a lily breasted on a lake
Grows fair from bud to petal, to herself
The law and reason for her coming forth,
So flowers existence from the original Soul.
Albeit she seem but a mysterious shade,
What lips would be her exorcist and purge
Away her glorious semblance from the mind ?
In arms of this divine Illusion rocked,
The manchild, firstling of the incarnate Soul,
Makes round his infant cycle, crescent thence
From type to type of personality.

Behold, a hope is born, a faith perceives,
Flaming sublime above her confines vast,
The advent of a purer day, when man
Will cast no shadow, but a thing of light
Essential, mingle gently, a clear beam,
With that which knows no change ; a day when she,
Her mighty task complete, will be withdrawn,
Her heart be stilled, her awful altars dimmed,
Her universal wheels, from which the suns
Leap up and sparkle till the eons fail,
Be stayed, and all her multitudinous lamps
Extinguished, silenced her harmonious choirs,
And this infinitude, furled like a scroll,
Depart, and through the shoreless void be rolled
A calm, majestic, everlasting Sea,
Life."
              While they mused upon his earnest words,
With eyes that singled Vivian, he resumed ;
" My son, my heart beats with you.   'T is my hope
To see your shackles loosened ere I die.
Much would I say that may not now be said.
And I would have you first assuage your heart
From these cool wells of beauty, hold the palms
Of nature for a season in your own.
You shall forget the world from which you came,
And what it thought or taught or sanctified,
Till all the tender faculties be ope
To spiritous omens, for a loftier lore
Ripe.   Tokens from the infinite, fine words,
Upon aerial anvils forged, will come
From bird and flower.   And mirrored in your eye,

The wide translucency of air, the mild
And crystal motions of the bounteous skies,
The unfathomable ether and the stars
Will be to you a prophecy, a voice
Of duty and monition.   You shall know
The starry throes of ecstacy, your mind
Be an angelic clearness, till you scale
The shining peaks of holiness and catch
The perfect Loveliness that lights the world."

And Vivian said, " O master, take my heart,
Shape, temper it to some celestial use,
And you of all men will I most revere.
Break up this vaulted darkness and insphere
A star within me that will never pale.
Far off the jangled hearts and creeds of men !
For I to-day have felt, the mind has seen
What may not be forgotten.   'T is my faith
That whoso has with open eyes beheld
Beauty, the universal light of God,
And loved her through some hours of passion, he
Can never wholly fail to what he was.
O spirit, come from skyey chambers down,
In full sereneness of that gentle light
Whereof our lives do suffer poverty.
Thy smile is on us and our hearts are glad ;
It passes, and we perish.   Elevate
Thy children that they be not all too low,
For they are of thee and their thoughts expect
Thy summons unto higher worlds of faith,
Thy revelation of diviner grace."

But then the prying sun forced them to hide
Deep in a fairy dell whose burnished sward
Titania's bridal slipper might have pressed
Uncrinkled and untarnished.   And therein
A clarion brook rustled his minted marge,
Wreathing soft folds of music around plots
Of sedge and osier.   Here two rills were joined
With laughter and a hoary oak hung out
A leafy screen to shield their married loves.
Delicious as the pearly depths that shone
In Agannippe or cool Hippocrene
To Hesiod panting from his morning walk,
Were thy translucent waves, O brook, to them.
They spake of Alpheus and his Aretheuse,
Called you more happy, praised the mixing lights
Of pebbles that veneered your paven floor,
Agate and turkis, jasper, emerald.
They prayed the quicks to weave their tasseled arms,
To knit their tendrils to a trellis cool,
Above, to save your cheeks from drouthy suns ;
Besought the mountains from their inmost hearts
And with perennial floods to feed your veins.
They drank, and laved their eyes and cheeks and
            brows,
Charmed from their feet the arrowy aches in baths
Of fresh medicinal foam, and lingered long
In dalliance with the pert capricious curls
Of this arch-wanton, fretted his sweet chime
To baby petulance, then fled his ire,
Refuged in mimic fortresses whose walls
Were overhung with rose-belled honey-suckle,

Their domes inlaid with roses.   Just o'erhead
One tiny throat shaped little pearls of song
And tossed them in their laps to win their grace,
As one who showers most cunning chivalries
Upon a stately lady proud in heart,
Who will not mark them.   Until Vivian said,
" O Paul, you only of us all can frame
Befitting answer to the gleeful bird.
I pray you, sound a note or two of rhyme,
And sing it to her."
          And Paul said, " I would
I knew to couch some happy word of thanks
In accords which her tender soul might read.
But this not I, nor subtlest bard of men.
I ween it is the self-same bird that piped
One mellow afternoon the while I strolled
These glades and made a poem.   As it grew,
Grew the bird's note in sweetness, keeping tune
With what I fashioned, and when the last verse
Ripened and dropped from where it hung upon
The branching fancy, lo, the gentle down
Had ceased to tremble on the weary throat,
And lifting up the dainty foot and wing,
She dipped down yonder odorous aisle to meet
Dun twilight stealing inward from the east."

Then Vivian, " Sing to us the rhyme you made,
For sure we will not stir until we hear."
And Arthur lifted a loud voice and cried,
" The rhyme, the rhyme or nothing, yea the
      rhyme."

And Paul leaned backward on the grass and sang
Softly in answer to the gleeful bird.

> Pour, pour the quivering streams
> Of thy liquid mirth around us,
> Kindle us with thy strong passion
> Ere the vesper chill hath found us ;
> Fling, fling in kingly fashion
> All the largess of thy dreams.
> Lo, the sweet eye-floods are dashing
> Hither from the solar fountain,
> Soar, soar, and in the brightness
> Steep the soft plumes of thy lightness ;
> Roll thy rounded harmonics,
> Weave thy wildest minstrelsies,
> Till the throbbing of thy gladness
> Tune the earth and touch the skies,
> And the woodland, mead and mountain
> Sing and dance in answering madness.
>
> What unknown fount of melody,
> What secret soul of piety
> Supplies the trembling of thy throat
> With the fashion of its note ?
> To what high haunt of glee
> Is access granted thee ?
> What cunning alchemy of speech
> Can guess the mixing of thy sweet ?
> What fine geometry can teach
> Thy mystic privilege to mete ?
> Wondrously thy thread is spun

From grain of rock, from waves of motion,
And somehow thy voice is one
With wail of wind and boom of ocean.
Thou bringest from the infinite
Under thy wings a message of light,
Could we but solve thy oracle
By spell or charm or miracle.

What doth ail thy note, strange spirit?
Fails it from thy deep desire?
Doth it flutter, pause and languish
From an inner strain of anguish,
That would crush and overbear it?
O wherefore load the crystal air
With pleadings so impassionate,
Who taught thee failings of despair,
Or bade thee murmur at thy fate?
Can thy fancy guess a higher
Than the bough where hangs thine ærie,
Or the cloud whose amethyst
Tangles thy plumes in webs of mist,
Till thy sprite is dark and weary?
But as thou singest, such am I.
For what it means I cannot tell;
A sorrow and an ecstasy,
A sigh of some strange melody
That floats and dies and all is well;
A fragment of the eternal Love
That chants around us and above,
That waves celestial pinions o'er us,
And sounds the trump of hope before us.

Quitting these genial boughs they homeward strolled
The bosom of a valley deep embowered
'Twixt guardian lengths of mountain, to itself
Shut in from prospect of the neighboring world,
Save where the cliffs that closed at either term
Left windows for the sun's first orient beam
And his last lingering glances from the west.
Wrapt in a summer mantle all of green,
Stirred here and there in little folds, she seemed
A baby princess stolen by monstrous elves,
Who while they bore her from her father's courts
Slept smiling in their arms.   Her wood-haunts wild
Had lured young Aphrodite scarce to miss
Her Paphian bowers, nor wooed Arcadian pipes
With pastoral warblings more soft-breathing slopes,
Or lawns more soothing sweet.   The nestled cot
From under flowery thatches peeped and laughed,
Round which the frolic brood of children danced
Like nursling robins fluttering nigh their nest.
Midmost within this garden of delight
They chanced upon a mansion quaintly built,
Rusted with years ; a mossy roof engrailed
With antique gables ; twilight porches gloomed
From brows down which the innumerable rose
Flooded the torrent blossom in full blush ;
An orchard here, and there a liberal square
Of garden, scored with tottering trellises
O'er which the lush vine loosed her leafy hair ;
A hedge of prickly stems, where of all hues
The mixing berries matched their rival charms ;
And full in front a lawn, in merest slope

Descending, spread her mats of green, o'erboughed
By altitudes of vast centurial elms.

" Here oft I came," the Master said, " in **days**
On which the aged heart more fondly dotes
Than years that followed after, to pursue
Juvenile pranks and games among the trees.
Then all was brighter, things were not so grey ;
And everywhere you met a graceful hand
Of neatness.   Here four stalwart striplings throve,
And spurned the sward with steps as light and **sure**
As the wild stag that roved our borders then.
The father, given to science and the books,
Helped on by native aptitudes in all,
Drew them to learning with so light a hand
They hardly felt the stress or fought with it.
But all were diverse.   Burke I never loved,
The eldest, hardest, all his words compact
Of arrogance and the affirming clink.
The vaguest topic broached, he lifted up
A front of contradiction harsh and bold.
The thing was never told till he had hacked
Some gashes in it, carved on it his mark,
Or smoothed it with a last complacent touch.
But well he could support at airy poise,
Move in swift circle, point in quarte and tierce
The dialectic blade, which he knew well
To burnish at his leisure.   Riper grown,
He chose the metaphysics and equipped
With such assiduous, comprehending thoughts
His mind with all the weapons of his art,

So shone with wisdom, as a tree that flares
A million icy spangles in the sun,
They sought him to adorn some famous chair
Where meek-browed scholars flocked with looks of
        awe.
Placid o'er vulgar hopes and fears, his brow
Not passion nor sweet sympathy could mar.
Buoyed upon eagle wings he compassed all
The lesser heavens and the round of time.
With necromantic wand well-armed, he oped
Secretest world-deeps by abstruse command ;
Guessed all the mundane riddles dark and fine ;
Systems, beliefs, primordial mysteries
Were clear as noonday to him.   He untied
Gordian subtleties and reconciled
By logic things deemed paradoxical.
By luminous esoteric methods grand
He spelled the universal plan, and clothed
In spotless pedantry, mooted the things
Of destiny.   Think not that thus from hate
I paint him with derision, or from scorn
Of knowledge at her amplest, but with aims
Of warning to you, lest your hearts be mocked
By masters mastered by the thing they know,
Mouthing the chaff of time.   O wherefore fly
Afar to find the temple-steps of God?
Ascend the fiery meteor, with him wheel
Aloft through all his giant period
Abysmal, visit each sublime abode
Stellar or solar, but the quest is vain.
He finds the most who wisely waits at home.

Your spirit, it is fate ; your love the star
For which you course the arcs of heaven in vain.

" Next younger Willis, whom I might have loved,
More pitied as too dilettantè, slight,
Unpolarized to any scheme or hope.
Sipping of many founts he drank of none,
Though leaning most to art.   Too weak to get,
He scorned to keep, but having, all his soul
Was largess, largess.   Darling with his mates,
Boon, placable and guileless, if he slipped,
'T was frailty and not choice.   Gay in his mood,
Winning in mien and in his manners bland,
He charmed all hearts with gentlest courtesies,
Yet, in the deeper lore of friendship, poor.
Graced with a dallying wit, a warbling laugh,
His buoyance never drooped from sun to sun.
The tempest could not break him, for he spread
His wings upon its breath and with it sailed.
Not daring tasks of weight, he better loved
Dainty, fantastic, fine dexterities,
Would mimic, touch the flute or sound the harp,
Strike out a lyric, sketch a random scene,
Or woo perchance a higher Muse and teach
The canvass to repeat a favorite mood.
Nature in him failed in the summing force
Organic and the law of unity.
So was his life shorn of its lawful scope
By that which seemed its glory.

　　　　" And the third
Was Percy, glittering like a beauteous pard

Fresh from his Afric jungle, not half weaned
From his fierce gambol.   He by word and deed
Published to men so cunningly what he was,
That few conceived the reason, though all felt
The charm.   In some Olympic game all eyes
Had followed him, as trifling with the rein,
Careless of winning, and the thing he did ;
Easily foremost when his heart was stirred.
Noble in power, daring in his thought,
And of imagination most intense,
He toyed with knowledge as a winsome babe.
He heard some native thunders in his soul
Of a melody so deep that a fierce scorn
Grew in him for the little race of men
Bartering their hearts for dust.   But wild and strong
Another music fell upon his ear,
Not falling from the amber peaks of heaven,
But steaming balefully from underground.
To fulsome and imperious bursts it swelled,
Printing its thousand motions on his sense,
Sweetly soliciting his lighter moods,
Till all his soul was mellowed to its power,
And to its dread intent his mind inclined,
And to its maze and interchange of strains
His feet were given in a mysterious dance,
And he fell into darkness and was lost ;
Drifting upon the shoulders of the sea
As a lone ship whose pilot drops asleep,
Steering nigh poppied banks of strange sea-isle,
While all the heavens are low and without star.
And partly to disburden his dark mind

From a corroding inner sense of ill,
Maddened by hissings of the feathered shaft
Of slander, part, in that he could not bow
To studious leisure, commerce with the books,
Or silken prattle of the gay saloon,
He roamed from clime to clime o'er half the world,
Mingled with novel faces, alien hearts,
And helped the Grecian sword against the Turk,
Struck with the Druse for cedarn Lebanon,
And after many years came home to die,
All his great heart in ashes.   Woe to him,
Who, coasting round ideal havens, casts
No anchor, but with wistful gaze looks back
Across the perilous deeps he sailed with toil,
Perusing his white wake with doubtful eyes.
For him the tempest lurks, him the abyss
Shall strangle in remorseless arms.
      "The fourth,
Youngest and fairest of the brood, was Ralph,
The gentlest spirit, nearest to divine,
Sweetliest tuned to all melodious things
Of the few souls that have been dear to me.
His manhood, luminous with pearly light,
Shone out as mild as Plato and as grand.
A full-orbed phantasy with chastened ray
Mantled with a perpetual poesy
The earnest speech his reason loved to plan.
On so much falling off you might insist
As in Love's star wavering through dewy air,
Or smiling hill-tops quivering through haze.
So much he seemed to falter from the sure

Unswerving circle.   So much from his act,
Perchance, of faultless evenness was missed.
This was the earthly rustling of her robe
That seemed the error of his soul.   He had
His perfect splendor here, if any have.
The whispering wind yielded him holy stuff
To weave into his being and the brooks
With mystic voices told him deeper things
Than bard or prophet knows.   He sought his own,
And faltered not, nor was content with less,
Nor measured by the canons of the sense
The aerial scope he had, nor sought of all
His heavenly toil a mortal recompense.
But to the larger sequence, wise to keep
His ever widening purpose aimed, he stooped
To no inferior amity, but wooed
Beauty in her own home.   Yet he is fled,
And all are fled, and I alone abide
To wander like a ghost among the fresh
And blooming generations, but not long ;
I am grown prescient of an end not far."

While thus he span the thread of character,
They passed the western gorge and clomb a hill
Smooth-verdured, to whose foot the village stretched
A snowy hand to pluck the plenteous fruits,
The summer yielding of the land.   Its crest
Murmured with lofty oaks that spread old arms
Of benediction over a neat cot
Enringed with lilac.   Mounting they beheld,
Within a rose-plot, Edith, whose sweet smiles

Long since had thieved the passionate heart of Paul.
She propped a pale tube-rose whose fragile grace
Too eager winds had clasped ; her piteous eye
Quickened the pulses in its stem, her breath
Doubled the ripening fragrance of the bud.
O, who could paint her as she seemed to him !
Ah, to his eye the roses' wealth of hue
Was shamed by that one rose upon her cheek.
The spirit of the summer filled her eyes,
Deep fountains of a mild and dewy light :
Twin buds that sleep, half opened, cheek to cheek,
Were those soft-glowing lips, and round her chin
Gathered the subtly curving lines of grace
That mould and plump a taper pear.   He thought
The lily-rose less graceful from its stalk
Than from the snowy arching of her neck,
The splendor of her head.   But he not typed
By other loveliness the mystic swell
Of the rich bosom, musically heaved,
Nor the sunlight of smiles that wont to haunt
The sporting dimples of her faultless hand.
O not the fiery radiance of the night,
Sole-lighted by the eager-bosomed stars,
But hers that gentle fairness when the moon,
Crescent, makes mild the heavens with a serene
And planet-tempering beam.
                        She came with smiles
Of sweetest welcome, guiding them to taste
The cordial shadows of the oaks that swarmed
Like hiving bees through all their foliage.
And then appeared the mother with a cheek

Whose ripe and mellow autumn glow the frosts
Began to wither, and a brow now blown
To silver ripples by harsh winds of the world.
In thickest shade she spread the cloth and brought,
From privy cache or larder cool, the milk,
Fresh loaves and edged with curls of crispy crust,
Within, of snowy grain and tenderest comb.
But Paul, untouched by thirst or famine, strolled
Through nooks of gentian, jasmine, mignonnette,
Musing of Edith. Oft in balmy June
He traversed by her side the woods and glens,
Spying the plants in nice botanic quest.
And never flower so perilous in its perch,
Far out upon the arms of giant pine,
Or on the forehead of o'erbeetling crag,
Or floating midmost in rank-breathing marsh,
But he, with light or bold devising hands,
Would pluck it from its proud security.
And so through natural channels of approach,
The mountain myth, the woodland song, the book,
Debatings over order or cohort,
Or passing interchange of thought and wit,
Or ponderings of the riper intellect,
Stole up dear hours of closer confidence,
And bringing in their hands the buds of love.
By happy instinct lured he pushed his walk
Far past the garden as in twenty strokes
Of his lithe wings a robin glides, and heard
The silver patter of a spring, coy-couched
Mid coiling roots and fretty rocks, that shook
The crystal banner of a waterfall

To tempt the mowers from the sultry swath.
Lo, on its brink the form of her he sought,
Kneeling beside the pail she came to fill.
Handling with aimless touch the cocoa-shell
Worn smooth by contact with the lips of men,
She watched the cradled slumber of the pool,
While some delightful fancy from her shape
Beguiled its animation, so reposing
Gently upon itself with naiad grace.
And Paul, partly unriddling her sweet mood,
Paused, and with fond and reverent looks of love
Explored her flowing mould of artless art.
Did she but lightly stir, he could behold
A hundred radiant graces glance and fade,
Chasing themselves around the arm and neck
And shoulder, till they melted into rest.
Love-bold, he stole on slow unspeaking steps
Across the soundless velvet of the sward
And caught within the fount her drooping face ;
A rose full-blossomed that upon its spray
Stoops from the burthen of a fragrant heart.
Eyelids, declining low, veiled from her ken
The face of him who could not choose but smile
From utter admiration and delight.
" Lo, the one vision of my life, the soul
Of Beauty which my love has wooed in dreams."

Whereat keen-startled, up she rose with eyes
Brimming with sweet bewilderment and fear,
And all the crimson eddies ceased to haunt
The frighted cheek only to come again

With a redoubled and beseeching fairness.
But Paul flowed on as though he marked it not,
" I cannot help but fancy that the spring,
Divinely urged to incarnate anew
Her spirit to its full degree of grace,
Would find these features faultless to her mind.
And should some mythic metamorphosis
Befall yourself, I ween no fairer type
Would offer than this covert fountain, rich
Through all his lucid deeps with tranquil joy.
Your pardon, lady, that without your leave
I put to flight what seemed a happy dream,
But something stronger than I could gainsay
Ruled in my feet.   I guess the God was Love.
Fair women blossom under every sky,
But, Edith, none so fair as under yours.
This mountain air contains some quality
That deepens all the sunlight in the soul.
Another sun renews the day-spring, change
Is wrought into the twilight and the stars
Have other glances.   Through the enchanted land
A wondrous presence meets me as I move,
A dignity, a gladness and a grace,
A kind of music very calm and bland,
Lining the world with golden blandishment.
Yea, and this inner life of mine is stirred
By knowledge of some late descended power,
And shakes my pulses with melodious noise.
And who this mighty sorcerer may be,
I cannot fathom, if he be not Love."

As some light cloud that wanders nigh the dawn
Changes from rose to pink, from pink to white,
Then quickly mounts again the scale of hues,
So changed her cheek beneath his earnest parle
And eyes wherein the solemn light of love
Intensely dwelt.   But whether from a heart
Not all instructed in its own desire,
Or partly doubting if his words were feigned,
Perchance a pettish unextinguished spark,
Because he caught her while she mused of him,
Howbeit, her answer seemed to come from scorn.
" O sir, this is a stately compliment,
Wrought, as I guess, on dreamy college-lawns
When you discoursed in Roman sentences.
I pray you, weave not with such careful hands
The color and the woof of flattery.
My ears are rustic to these harmonics.
But yet, I thank you, lest your heart be vexed.
I know that often scholars from the town
Assume the cavalier and grow enamored
Of some fair Pastorella of the vale.
Doubtless it turns an after boast or two
When jocund comrades marshall their exploits."
But when she marked the pain within his eyes,
" Forgive me, Paul, I would not do you wrong.
I have believed you nobler."
                              Clearer then
Shone out his starry passion, and he said,
Cleaving her transient cloud of skepticism,
" Ah, all unjust to turn to passing jest
Words flowering on the very stalk of love.

It was my creed no woman breathed so fair
To charm my liking with this gentle case.
O trust me, Edith, that my love is great.
O trust me as a kind of rude completion,
The ambient and protecting husk wherein
Your tender ear may fill its golden glow,
Or a firm roof to fend perplexing gusts.
Trust in me, for I hold you as a saint,
Whom I would worship with best piety."

And a mild light of meekness on his face,
And passion-thrilling supplicating tones,
And memory, haply, of her bitter words
Smote her with quick contrition and the tears
Stole out upon the margins of her eyes ;
While musical and low the plaintive voice,
Woven with merest tremblings, answered him,
"O Paul, I little merit to be loved,
Interpreting with such ungracious eyes
The gift you proffer. But your heart is great,
Too great to parley with my idle spleen.
And if you find a worth in one like me,
So poor in brilliance, poor in all but love
And fond forecastings of an upward mind,
That would commeasure with you noble ends,
Lo, I will follow you through all the earth,
And if I cannot love you as I ought,
I will forever love you as I can."

Thus clear from her deep-fountained womanhood
Murmured the crystal wave of answering love.

And the transcendent flicker of a light,
Not born from any sun or star that shines,
Gleamed o'er the bowed and waiting face of Paul.
And he caught up her dimpled palm that nigh
For softness melted in his grasp and said,
"O Love, look up.   Behold heaven's star of Love
Steals into being from the evening splendor,
Twin-born with ours ; our chosen pilot-star.
And when his form is hidden in the skies,
We 'll find his perfect image in our hearts."

O rose and matchless fragrance of all hours,
When Love salutes us from a maiden's eyes,
And magic instincts stir and the young heart
Gushes in song !   O golden sum of all,
When two clear billows on the sea of Beauty,
Moved upon diverse but symmetric tides,
Break to each other o'er the rocky bars
Of personality, and, blending, bloom
Upward in a white foam of spotless passion !
Yet this is Love, the mystic elf, quick-born
Upon the tremulous bosom of a sigh,
A gleam, a glow, a fine and flitting pinion,
A liquid rhyme or young Titania's dream.
But lovers must aye purge their mortal selves,
Making their breasts clear shrines of crystalline,
That Beauty, from her lodge in either soul
Peeping, may quickly know herself and yearn
For that old oneness ere the man was framed.
The lovers are the chosen, unto them
The incommunicable is revealed.

Crisp brooks that wed in some Arcadian dell,
Paired throbbings of two happy throats in June,
Bright tints of morn that gently blend to one,
Marriage of sweetest sound with silentness,
These, these be lovers' spirits when they meet.

Paul filled the empty pail and they moved forth
Together, conning o'er in fragrant talk
The secret tale of love in either breast,
The thrillings of those precious pains and all
Delicious agonies that lovers know.
And passing down the garden-walk they found
Blossom and bud closing to tranquil dreams,
And one lone bee late-lingering at the rose.
They sought the oaks under whose sheltering boughs
The chatting throng were grouped on twisted chairs
In circle round the patriarchal sire.
And by him sat the son, easing his limbs
From labored furrows of the cloven grain.
Then as the evening fell, the Father raised
Their souls with meditative discourse mild,
And touching upon the advent of his death.
And all were charmed by a lone flageolet,
Tuned by some mournful villager, that seemed,
Unto pathetic fancies warbling low,
The burthen of the twilight hour wept down
In liquid melodies.   Long time it moved
Through soft imploring passionate desires,
Then flung its whole heart upward into heaven
In one wild surge of agony, and then
Fell down through cadences of deep despair

To fondle a serene regret and blend
Softly and softlier with the twilight hush.
All eyes were filled with tears, and, touched in soul,
They sat and watched the moon through plaited
        boughs
Spangle the sward with silver, leafy heights
Twinkle with fire-flies voyaging the night
With lamps that ever needed to be trimmed,
And spied careering bats carve on the sky
Their fitful lines, the while through all his stems
The broad catalpa nodded to the sound
Of cricket lullabies. From silver mists
That crept like luminous serpents down the vales,
The lonely owlet shot his clear too-whit,
And not the faintest murmur of a breeze
Disturbed the folded eyelids of the flower,
But over all, the mild and wide abyss
Of nature's motion and great silentness
Deepened in beauty and far in the north
The fiery shuttles, weaving up the night,
With sudden magic clothed the half of heaven
In robes of crimson, purple and of gold.

IV.

WHEN his downy sleep has ending,
Finds the wildered youngling there
No sweet presence o'er him bending,
Flower nor brook nor arbor fair.
Weird enchantment of a night,
Vanished is the semblance bright.
But above him breaks a light ;
Voiceless, shapeless, save a hand
Beckoning with august command.
Divine in clearness and severe,
Skyward it mounts in starry error ;
But he has no sense of fear,
And he loves it for its terror.
From him burgeon wings aerial,
Beat melodiously the breeze,
And he cleaves the far ethereal
Ocean with angelic ease,
Following that sign imperial.

Pompous rites not celebrate
Secret birthday of the soul,
When the first warm flush of fate
Crimsons her terrestrial feature,
And the waves of godhood roll

Gently round her mortal nature.
Only silence has perceived it,
Only God in heaven believed it.

But this dawning is the seal
Of her greatness, chosen thence
Child of Beauty. She shall feel
Nevermore the throes of sense,
But sweet pulses out of heaven
Shake her heart with motions even.
Though the laws and cycles sure
Fade like mist, she will endure.
For above the thunder-hum
Where hiving planets go and come,
Greater than the incarnate whole,
Lives and loves the Eternal Soul.

———◆———

By the reluctant paces of a stream,
Just where a recluse grove of willow loosed
Her lavish braids in golden cataract,
The wanderers, slanting from the tingling meads,
Flung down their drowsy limbs and drank the cool.
And here a church kept sanctuary dim.
All breathed with age and unresisted mould,
And lawn and walk betrayed neglectful hands.
The massy palings warped or fallen askance
From nails rust-eaten, from their sockets slipt,
Or spurned by myriad feet of heedless winds,
Tempted the roving steer's besieging horn
To force admittance to the solemn shades

And sacred pastures. And the temple rose
Compact in front and flank of dusky stones,
Whose swarthy cheeks, untamed by chisel, wore
With rugged pride their native mountain lines,
Or patched their scars with tattered breadths of moss.
Around the porch thick wefts of ivy clung,
From which a hundred tendrils, shooting, caught
The fretty eaves or up the gable glanced,
And peeped and dangled, and one spray of mind
More daring, scaled the summit of the cross,
And seemed to drag it somewhat from its perch,
Albeit it only toppled from its age.
Perusing the dark pile, the Master said :

" Even to the dawning eye of infancy
These battered walls seemed old and grey as now.
Dear is the memory of sweet Sabbath morns,
When, guided by the godly mother's hand,
I entered here and heard the shepherd warn
His simple flock, and mete with lowly hands
The ministration of the word divine.
Here the first pencil of supernal light
Played out of heaven upon my spirit, here
Took root within me the prime germ of all
That best my heart has since achieved. O blest,
Forever blest the shining hands of Her,
Great mother of a noble Titan brood,
Whose mild paps fed us ere the mind was ripe
To measure its desire ! Ah, now her voice
Fails from its melody, and her deep eyes,
Fountains of mourning, wander through all heavens

In hopeless imploration ; Niobe
Beseeching for her children, whom no more
Her great heart will caress.   In after youth
Some doubts, engendered in a lonely hour
Of meditation, hunted me like wolves.
And smit with agony by day and night
I wooed the solitude of yonder hills
Until my times were finished and the soul
Was purged of darkness.   But my mother wept.
She held it for a fearful sin and wept.
And with moist eyes of prayer she drew me where
Her wisdom had its fountains, and her faith,
The pulpit.   Here a noisy pulpiteer
Made havoc, and we heard the sacred themes
Parceled by theologic rule, with heights,
Compact of morticed logic, embattailed ;
Words rich in gleaming sallies, hot descents,
Keen arrow-flights transpiercing in their swoop
Hostility and every creed that blew
A trumpet and durst smite his rounded walls.
But I, imploring bread, received a stone.
Ah, when will one be found of worthy speech,
Unfolding the eternal word with fear,
Not adding and not dwarfing, reverent !
The time is sick at heart with vacant talk.
Wisdom takes perch upon the lips and thence
Fulmines, not knowing of the deeper soul.
The prophet is the speaker of the Word.
He bends his ear close to the whispering lips
Of nature and in holy melodies
Sings to the world the secrets she imparts.

Heavenborn ! we welcome thee with love and joy,
To whom the Great God has revealed himself."

And Vivian said, " More than Crotona old
Or Sais, or the lips of Pythia,
These wood-haunts promise to my thirsting mind.
For often under other skies than these,
Watching at eve some faintest star increase
From throb to throb its beauty till it shone
Naked, complete, the master of its course,
The weary heart would yearn for some great Seer,
A teacher who would plume my soul to mount
High past the turbid ether and alight
Upon the golden rind of some fair world,
A truth immortal as the star I saw.
In you my sigh is granted.   While you speak
My mood is lightened.   O speak on, for I,
More dutiful than Plato at the feet
Of him who greatly slighted to be great,
Attend.   I hang upon your tale of her,
This hoary mother of the centuries,
Herself a suckling from the mighty breast
Of that world-nurse, the Orient, old and grand."
      Whereto the reverent Master made reply ;
" Think not I would say aught in trivial scorn,
The foam of hearts not certain of themselves,
Of her who nourished me.   I rather keep
A veneration.   And her potent hands,
Her sovereign eyes and most resplendent brow,
Her world-embracing purposes and deeds
Lay hold upon me.   Into purer types

From age to age ascending, she fulfils
Alway an ampler duty. Often soiled
O'er all her glorious features with the mire
Of worldliness, and many times eclipsed
By thunder-darkened tempests from her prime
Sweet sanctity of adoration, lo,
She has from error still reclaimed her feet
And taken a new brightness. But behold,
Her much-supporting knees do crumble ; all
Her offices grow languid in the pulse.
No more for her the courts of heaven, no more
The master-sway of mightiest emperies.
A greater far than she rises to snatch
The falling sceptre. Exiled long, he comes,
Young Jove, full-grown upon the secret sweets
Of Ida, and the feeble dynasties
Shake to his footing. The young soul of man,
No longer abject, cowering far from sight,
Puts on the gleaming armor of assault,
And summoning those proud powers, which he rules,
Moves to his realm of Beauty. Unto all
New hope is added. This humanity,
That might spread sail upon eternal seas,
A long time stranded on the shores of Time,
And like a wounded sea-bird wildly wailing,
Far-peering in the dim abysses, cried
For God. For her no comfort could be found.
But now the Ideäl, fluttering past her eyes
On white-winged light divine, renews again
Her spirit. She will knit the sundered beams
And trim her masts, taking for pilot one

Who finds his star within him, inly urged
By bold creative insight self-sustained.
Restored to kinship of the elder gods,
No more she plies the supple knee, the fool
Of mortal doctrine, sold to symbols, once
Meet poesy of largest utterance,
Now vacant of their beauty, being misused ;
From hintings of an arduous piety
Degenerate to civic uses grown,
And tricked in gauds, wooing the childish eye.
But nay, we wrong not beauty anywhere.
Within her folds yet linger noble hearts,
Not all oblivious of the trust they bear.
Like fragrant gardens sown in withered lands,
Or cool-veined fountains amid torrid wastes,
Nursing a hermit verdure, is this true
And spotless brotherhood of God, who strive
To sweeten a sour age with holy lives."

And Paul said, " O let come the riper day !
Great dawn, uplift with speed your awful head,
Pour forth your crimson seas !   A few, with eyes
Of worship, watch the slowly orbing hour.
What though the world with blindness reels !   O yet
A hundred Phosphors call you from your bed,
Dear queen Aurora !   For your eyes we thirst.
O touch the hills with glory, come and crown
The deeps with warming blush and bathe in fire
The valleys whence the night lifts slowly ! Come,
Another race will greet you, other hopes."

The Sire smiled on him as he made response.

"Young spirits nurse the buds of fairest schemes.
Yet be not too enamored of your wish,
Nor limn too generously with glorious traits
The coming time, lest adverse omens taint
With bitterness the sweetness of the heart.
I praise the man whose eye has well discerned
The majesty and the transcendent worth
Of the Necessity which pilots all.
The weak are ground to powder by his feet,
But the bold-hearted are his darling sons.
Love well the great Necessity, on him
Pillowed in love, the soul as gently sleeps
As babe in cradle.   Much we trust will come.
Enough to catch the moments as they fall
And speak the truth revealed from hour to hour.
Not ours to lightly mock the bruited past,
From whom the thought is fledged and taught to soar,
But rest firm-grounded on the present, still
Our door ajar to tempt the future in.
O not the trump of war, nor statutes forged
Upon the anvil of authority
By haughty guardians of the common-weal,
So teach the world to dare the forward track,
As the pure voices of her noble sons,
Who, moving far before her up the heights,
Summon her on with those melodious peals,
Resistless in their sweetness.   Oft, in sooth,
The song is more fulfilling than the law."

Then Arthur slipped a wave that chafed his heart.
"Reformers east, reformers west, to south

Reformers.   O my Paul, I love you well.
But wiser, I opine, the enginry
Of staidest wont, of firm-set church and state,
Contentious sect, or caucus in the dark,
Than roseate eras you invoke to turn
All topsy-turvy this fine house of cards.
I rather cry with him who in his tower
Shuffled the world in quartoze or capot,
'*Que sais-je,*' see-saw with truth from morn to eve,
Than split these steadfast bergs and drift their floes
By mole and pier with ruin.   Do you wince?
I would conserve.   Firm ground is dear to feet
That will stand sure.   But you pull down the hills
And leave us painted clouds, raze battlement
And tower to build fantastic shapes of air.
Yet speak, my Thalaba, what recompense,
What law to guide, when all this change is wrought?

"Love," echoed Paul, with eyes that burned like
        stars,
"Love, stronger than your civic bolts and bars,
Love, wiser than your banded Israel,
Full Love, and templed in the breasts of all.
Is this too far, too arduous?   O hush!
Hast sounded all the height and depth of the soul?
Hast weighed it in the hollow of the hand?
Take heed, the ground is holy where you tread!
All hear the wind, the earthquake and the fire,
Fewest the voice, still, small."
                And Vivian said,
"Each has his faith in man, but diverse.   I

Have this creed yet to fashion. I have heard
Alway the voice of pity sound his dirge ;
Swart wen upon creation ; the sole shaft
From all God's quiver that has missed its aim."

Then spake the Master, his benignant face
A little kindled from its wonted calm,
" Great bards, their wings upon immortal themes
Loftily buoyed, have compassed heaven and earth
To gather golden stuff from which to weave
Proud eyries on the highest peaks of song.
Their ears, low-couched, have caught with breathless
         awe
The stately whisper of an elder day,
Or their prophetic hands have sought to mould
The hours with which the present hour is big.
Men they have fashioned, heroes to their minds,
Forgers of fate, masters from their first breath,
Fierce hearts and smoking swords and maths of death :
Or, lured by gentler fancies, have passed through
The worlds of faery, seats of vanished gods,
Plucking a wisdom from abandoned mines,
Shaping their path by glowworms in the dusk,
Or stars of song in mythic twilight hung.
And they have cleft hell open to the core
And watched her black heart pulsate without guise ;
Or, past the utmost zenith shooting, turned
The pearly portal on harmonious hinge,
Paced up and down the heavenly aisles and heard
Symphonious bursts, a million strains commingled.
But who with fond imagination, love

Unutterable and fearless thought sublime,
Has sung your greatness from a burthened heart,
Dear child of wonder, darling of the sphere,
Majestically lifting your white brows
Betwixt the morning and the evening star?
The most have partly wronged you, meting out
A niggard honor, more your shame than praise.
For whence shall hope be drawn but from within?
Or who will base his logic for man's worth
On other than his freedom and intense
Endeavor that persists unto the end?
Humanity, decrepit in the will,
Leans forward, blindly groping for a prop,
Faithless that the great soul is all in all.
Yourself unto yourself are infinite,
Or else are nothing. Wherefore weakly heed
Dissonant echoes of an age confused,
Whose teachings rustle like to withered leaves
Whirled into eddies by a wintry wind!
O the rich mystery of the soul we bear,
Unfathomed, widening till it weds with God!
It takes, it gives, it is the only lord.
It deals our measure of the infinite,
Is past and present and what is to come.
It is the man and world, the God and heaven,
And when interpreted by poets' eyes
And made externe and fixed in during forms
Of beauty, which alone it deigns to wear,
The earth is peopled with the things it names
Divine, the philosophic and the good,
The musical. The soul is fount of all.

Shall hope unfurl his purple vans and steer
With happy throbbings to celestial bournes,
Only to welter amid cloudy drifts,
And burden all his plumes with mortal tears,
His ardor quenched in darkness ?   Shall the voice,—
The prayer, the lamentation and the pain,—
That rises from a thousand lips debased
In the dust of time, its suppliant agony
Prolong forever, and no more appear
Bold foreheads tameless to disastrous shocks,
Clear-beaming eyes and manly rhythms that hymn
The lofty harmonies of life and love,
Valor and labor and victorious hands ?
O not to writhe in ashes and defile
His glorious locks, to waste divine desires
In childish penance and ungracious grief,
Was this fair star of God's humanity
Born from the abyss and taught to rise and set,
And, clothed with awful beauty, shine and sing.
But greater than the weakness and the shame,
And strong to slay the myriad-twining ill,
Man will arise, inspired by earnest thoughts,
To roll the anthem of a lordlier faith,
And follow with a conscious will that knows
Its greatness, all the purposes august
That he, urged to the height of his estate,
May handle and create."
    And Paul, aglow,
Caught up the pregnant theme in passionate hands.
" This is the only hero whom I love :
Alway his princely features haunt my eye.

He wears the weight of life with royal ease :
The cloudy flutterings of the raven night,
Stretching her ebon wings to cover up
The golden circle of his starry aim,
Conspire alone his beauty to increase.
He asks not of the scornful world an alm,
Whose clamors cannot ruffle the repose
That, like eternity, within him sleeps.
He knows a fountain set in amaranth,
Whereof who takes can neither bate nor fall,
But a most subtile alchemy can wield,
That, solving hostile forces, leaves him free.
Albeit he blend not with the dust and roar,
Hedged round with lonely thinkings, neither dull
The spirit's fine-wrought edge against the crust
Of the world, nor count it gain to pluck
The bloom of social culture, rude to play
The prank of vulgar splendor, yet he finds
A guerdon purchased not by gold or gems.
For what his hands accomplish shall endure
And burgeon into vaster, till it bless
All afterbirth ; yea, the clear rays he shoots,
Rounding the crescent into star, will flow
In tides of broadening lustre till they bathe
All peaks and plains, the desert and the deep.
The years march to the music of his voice,
The seasons gather brightness and the sun
Radiance, and all the starry throngs rejoice,
Since he has sung.   So cunning is his lay,
Barbaric fancies quicken, and the hordes
Stream from their lairs in cavern and in crag.

His lips repeat with sweetest Orphic ease
The old, divine, eternal melodies
To which the timbers of the world were laid.
Stern nature from her stubborn mood is tamed,
Her pliant feet dance round in mazy rings.
Courage is his to trust his vision, speak
Relentlessly the law he finds and aye
Maintain to it his loyalty.   Against
His mind severe and glowing love avail
Nothing the velvet palms of fondling fame.
But on the pompous semblance and the false
Supremacy he pauses not to urge
The shining terror of his arm."
          He breathed.
But Arthur gibed at his oracular heat;
" O Paul, you fling your colors out so broad,
So lavish of grand lines in what you draw,
You seem to hit the moral gigantesque.
I miss the mortal mixture that would stir
My love and tears and make me feel him **man.**
As Byron paints a devil, you a saint.
Good men are well, so they be flesh and **blood,**
But I love not these pampered idolisms.
Not stocks nor stones nor hardened Stoic **brawn,**
The icy sheen, fixed eye and marble brow,
Pitiful continence of frozen hearts,
Can teach my blood new fire.   O these serene
And polished dignities that look the god !
Were I for one day Jove I 'd brush my hand
Across the world and tumble from their seats
Some score of them.   My soul would shake **her sides**

To mark them beat the dust from their soiled robes,
And reinstate their crowns.   O pish, not I
Immaculate, I love a fault or two.
Better the blow struck daringly, though vain,
Than sword forever rusting in the sheath."

Paul laughed.   But Vivian from the minted grass
Rose half and loosed his volley of protest.
" I ween some harder blows are struck in the world
Than these you wot of, Arthur.   Fie on you,
To dash your inky pot of cavil thus
Across these stately features.   While you prune,
You thrust the blind knife through the root of all.
These lofty virtues pillar and adorn
The very temple and the soul of man.
Tug not to loose them : if they fall, yourself
Are crushed beneath the ruins.   But you love
From ways of contradiction, nursed of old,
To don the sable vizard of a mood
Not native to you ; overfond to flout
At what your truer heart extols as fair.
This time go free : take heed to sin no more."
All smiled at Vivian and he at himself,
Then said, " O Master and O Paul, beloved,
You fanned me into life of purer flame.
The childish ardor dies, the man arrives,
The symbols flee, but he whose wand invoked,
Their master and great Prospero, abides.
I pant for this large freedom in the soul."

And as he spake, gleams of peculiar joy

Played o'er the wrinkles of the Father's face;
A sire who smiles on some beloved child.
And lifting up his serious voice he said,
" The worship native to the child as blood,
Self-prodigal and barren of the force
That wisely will regard and disregard,
Too oft deals forth its costly gifts amiss.
But riper years are missioned to impart
A due subjection and due sovereignty.
This insight and full freedom will be yours :
But none may witness their benign approach,
Which eye of man has never seen, his ear
Heard never : a dew-fall, a plume of light,
A trance, they come.   And somewhat as a child,
Amid the daily teachings of the hearth,
Parental accents, tongues of blithe compeers,
From the heart of the inarticulate confines
A language, a sweet miracle of speech,
Which each ensuing year nurses to form,
So wins the soul her secret certainty.
Heed well, my son, the words I speak.   Belief
That marches to fulfil itself must wield
The weapons of no unheroic valor.
Wisely deny.   So has true freedom birth.
Hearts strong to break from vain and solemn shows,
Unto the strait prescript and feeble sense
Of alien doctrine never bow, but seek
A revelation in themselves of peace
And harmony.   Then make the spirit bold.
Servile is fear and blind to the vast love,
That shines from nature with perennial beams.

Gleaned from all times, the purport of the man
Is but to pass with toil from point to point,
Finding, attaining, firmly based on love,
Which is the first and final of all laws.
Wherefore denial, yoked with fear, is death.
Sit, while the wondrous fabric of the race
Disjoints itself before the tranquil eye,
And every passing sect disclosure makes
Of its ambition.   Let it rule or sink,
The earth feels not the shock beneath her rind.
You falter to accept the permanence
Of this or that.   I say to you, doubt all,
And have them render witness of themselves.
Shake off the burdens of the centuries ;
With every man begins the world anew.
But whoso will uplift a suppliant hand
To smooth a ruffled God with many prayers,
Stuffed with repentance that goes forth in groans
And steeps the bruised soul in baths of tears,
Barren of good, but whets his pangs anew.
Vain is the melting heart and upward steam
Of lamentation.   You shall be compact
Of fortitude and of enduring power ;
Until upon the horny surge of fate
Your head be pillowed as on summer moss,
And when his joints asunder seem to fall,
And all his limbs are writhed in agony,
The soul may hold her scornful merriment,
And on the dancing gulfs established be,
As on the centre of the world.   For aye
Lives and works-on the prime celestial law,

Whose golden wheel is irreversible.
Therefore no murmurs, neither clasp of palms,
Nor faint nor spasm within, but evermore
The calm expectance of the mighty hope
That looks unto an end which cannot fail."

But at these words severe the tender cheek
Of Vivian paled, his soft eyes shone with tears,
And all his voice was broken as he said,
" Ah, Master, set me not a task too hard.
My soul is timorous of herself and all.
These words you speak are terrible : I seem
An atom banished from the face of light,
Cleaving in cheerless flight a pitchy void,
Defeated, base, deform, accurst, eclipsed,
Hunted by fierce disdain from gloom to gloom.
May I, the weakling of a summer hour,
Sound bold defiance at the gates of heaven ? "

" Ah, faithless," said the Master. " It is writ,
Heaven's kingdom is within you. Know full well,
Yourself are portion of the builded All,
Brother to what you seek. O then weep not
Like a weak babe within its nurse's arm,
That clings, and will not nestle in the breast
The mother offers, knowing not her face.
March forward, hopeful of the time to come,
And what you sought without, seek now within.
You shall envisage the unchanging Soul
With unimaginable splendor girt,
Play with her terrors lovingly and bathe

In all her fiery deeps, for she is yours
And never can be taken.   O dream not,
'T is given to scale the crystal walls of heaven,
And with familiar eyes to contemplate
The eternal forms in naked majesty ;
Nor yet to guess the puzzles of the world
By slow ascensions of imperious thought ;
Nor boldly spying out the secret halls
Of Knowledge, to behold her eye to eye.
But Love is yours ; gracious interpreter
Of the great silence and the mystery.
All victory has nature with an oath
Given to the soul that fearlessly obeys
Her inmost law of love.   And Love is but
The Soul's divine acquaintance with herself.
Be not the fool of time.   But rather know
Illusion harbors in the eye that sees,
And from the unconscious mind his currents flow.
Whose converse is with shadows, by degrees
Is turned to shadow, and his folly names
The world a potter's vacant trick.   Purge then
The mind.   Lift it to overpeer the peaks
Of time and sense, to where mid awful rays
The uninvested Truth unsearchably
Reposes.   Cast aside these weights of doubt.
Trust the great God that he is good and fair
With inexpressive beauty.   Break the band
That hinders, and surrender and forget ;
For these prelude the heaven-illumined eye,
The aspiring hope pinioned with starry fire,
The consecrated heart, the holiness,

Divine revealments, satisfying peace.
Once islanded upon itself, the mind,
No more a shifting Delos, is bound fast
To the firm world and on its margins roll
The waters of the everlasting sea,
The thunder and the mighty harmony.
But ah, my son, all words are broken hints
Which life adjusts to a significance.
Yet these may prompt you in secluded hours
To toil without remission. Largelier
My heart desires to speak the pregnant lore
Of culture and a greater far than she,
Reverence, and haply will before I die.
And so, perchance, if you fail not in power,
Nor, slumbering, forego the constant eye
Of holy vigilance, you will achieve
Intelligence of the Divine and win
A high, imperishable goal. And then
Lift up thanksgiving and a voice of praise.
For who has held this knowledge, though he lose
Its quickening presence for a season, yea,
Although the dark floods whelm him for an age,
Alway retains a lofty memory
That through the foam and clamor bears him up
To be that force he has been and may be.
O yet, beware the common and the base,
Lest adverse fate, born of the recreant soul,
Work through all elements and accidents,
Empoison the sweet air and thieve away
The sustenance of purposes divine,

Yea, marring the prime splendor of its hope,
Topple the spirit into gulfs of night."

Then Vivian, re-emboldened and consoled,
Lifting his eyes from their abasement, smiled,
And to the Master said, " Great thanks I owe
For these unfoldings.   Like a rock that feels
The throes of Phœbus' lyre, my heart perceives
Harmonious motions, instincts that presage
Triumph and sweetest reconcilement there.
'T is true that many shadows are withdrawn.
Enough, enough of dead mechanic days,
Of visual strivings touching transient ends,
Of sowing golden ends on barren sands.
But if there be some Good will never pass,
Some mountainous pillar firm amid the flood
Of that which, ever seeming, still must seem
The faithless figment of a deeper seeming,
Surely its lodgement centres in the soul.
O then no more the footless thought, no more
Anguish of warring fancies.   I will be
Swift to forsake, encounter and endure,
Earnest to listen, instant to believe
Monitions that have there their birth."
                              And Paul
Leaned over and kissed Vivian on the cheek,
And said, " O friend, I will repeat a strain
A fair star gave me while I watched his steps
At midnight."   And he turned upon his back,
Fixed his blue eye on heaven and thus began :

O well for him, whose spirit, wise
Above the mortal jar and bruit
Of seeming evils that impute
Discord to the designing skies,

Beholds the large necessity,
And each upon his starry road,
The shining periods of God
Complete themselves in majesty;

Unharmed and undiminished, whole;
Infecting wild and baser forms
With their endeavor, as the charms
Of Orphic lute all natures stole.

Calm-hearted, as his trust is deep,
This one has amplitude of scope,
Even to the measure of his hope,
Because august Desire will keep

True to her proper ordinance,
No longer threading ways of mire,
Nor scorched in lonely lands of fire,
Nor drifted on the tides of chance.

And his achievement as a brook
Simple and pure and joyful runs,
Courts not acclaim of praise, nor shuns
The gorgon worldling's whetted look.

This the true sage who can postpone
The lesser gain that turns by use

Into a seed of worst abuse,
Whose name is death, when fully grown,

Unto the lordly aftergood,
That comes with clouds of radiance,
Wearing a glorious countenance,
To every soul of noble mood.

But ill for him who thrusts a hand
Itching with thirst of base increase
Among the sweets while yet the bees
Come in thigh burdened from the land.

He gathers loss and bitter pain.
O trust the years, they will achieve
A fairer than thy dream and weave
An ampler heaven, more pure of stain.

Let ripen that which grows.   Debar
No crescent blossom from its girth
And golden finish, which the earth
Gives to her chosen with fond care.

Yet temper so thy shaping power
That each endeavor may be rife
With the one spirit of thy life,
And hour be kin to rolling hour.

Ah, he forestalls all increment,
Who counts the years of worth to hide
The steppings of unlawful pride
With splendor false and transient.

Let the eye range.   Behold afar
A clearness on the brow of night,
The tempest's wing aglow with light,
Born from the wheels of some grand star.

Let the eye range.   Behold the Deep
Slowly retires her mutinous heads,
While all along her million beds
The soul of Chaos lies asleep.

Let the eye range.   Lo, the wise fate
Brings from the thunder and turmoil
With method sure and patient toil
Something of beautiful and great.

When down his slope ecliptic fallen a third,
The sun shot forth a drouthy glare, they rose,
And keeping alway round them cloaks of shade,
Thridded the land in talk of easier pitch ;
Skimming with fitful wing a shifting theme,
But hovering with most glee about the skirts
Of science ; spake of bulb and bract and whorl,
Sessile or petiolate ; pelted the rocks
With studious malice, rhomb or cube or prism,
Calc, talc, or sphene, pyrite or malachite ;
Or broached the polar drifts with theory ;
Or stumbling on a fossil, talked of shell,
Saurian or mastodon.   Anon they met
A fairy burg sequestered.   Towering rocks
Precipitous, with ominous ledge and cliff

Impending, dangled wreaths of ruin down
Above her.   Yet she wore a smiling look,
A feature of security.   They heard
The muffled murmur of the mill, the boom
Of mellow waters, where before his breast
The weir abrupt held out a sheeny targe ;
And saw how, moaning like Ixion old,
The brook, beneath remorseless paddles crushed,
Dragged out his mangled limbs in tortuous foam,
Where moved the monstrous wheel in lazy gyre.
Farther, they spied a cottage large and quaint,
Brown as the crags, yet breathing out a grace,
A meekness and a purity, within
The dusky circle of an elm whose top,
A cloud of green hung in the azure, drooped
Through all its languorous fringe.   Hard by the cot
A sooty stithy clamored with the sledge,
And thick-lunged bellows creaked with every blast.
There nodding in an oaken chair asleep,
They saw a form under the latticed arch
That screened with plaitings of luxuriant vine
The lintel.   And they named him, in a trice,
The white-haired Vulcan of the vicinage ;
Grey Colossean ruins of a frame
That might have borne the thunder-shocks of great
Alcides' heart.   Under his load of snows
He bowed, a Titan sunk beneath the weight
Of the thunder, the severe Atlantian ridge
Of the sloped shoulder scarred and crushed ; the mail,
Seen through the wide-flung collar on his breast,
Close-linked and massive o'er the antique breadth,

Deep-dinted from a hundred jousts of life ;
The mighty jaw unstrung and the strong eyes
Aweary, far retired within their caves,
O'er which the shagginess declined.   He rose,
Catching their steps, and motioning salute
Came slowly forth and grasped the Master's hand ;
And for a space these hoary Pillars rose
In strange conjunction, beacons of a world
Long vanished.   While the Three made lowly signs
Of meet obeisance, lo, he turned and caught
Their hands in welcome, led them in and said,
Ethan, the Smith, " Come sit, my lads, and share
My shade here.   Let me look into your eyes.
Heigh-ho, it helps my age to have the beams,
The clear straight lightning of untaméd youth,
Strike full upon me.   From your cheeks, heigh-ho,
My soul sucks out a purple that will cheat
This death that hunts me of a day or two.
We had a whisper of you,— three strange lads,
Striplings from college, visiting the Hills.
You 're packed with learning, as I read your brows,
Ay, and I mark the studious languor too
Of the upper eyelid ; but in you, meseems,
A sadness, sir, a trouble in the eye.
What, do you bury here some fresh love-scorn,
The poutings of disdainful lady there?
O nay, no maiden lives so rude to slight
This constellation of fair attributes
Disclosed upon your face.   By Thor, I have
A brace of cubs as rough to grapple with
As e'er were welded of our highland brawn ;

But heigh-ho, lad, God bless me, they to you
Are the bulked pines that surge their unkempt curls
About our ledges, to the airy mast
That bends a graceful neck above the lake.
Nay, lad, I speak my heart out, what it feels."

And Vivian laughed and said, " Better to rove
A lion's whelp, the master of the plains,
Than drowse beside a kennel though in thralls
Of silk.   Ye are a better folk than we.
Your marrow holds some grains of granite, we
Are but the pulp and down of things.   Your heart
Drives the sure shock to brain and palm from year
To year undaunted, and ye put to task
Nature herself to keep your souls at bay.
Ye out-fate fate and lead him by the beard,
Are storm and sunlight, with your seasons fixed,
A part of all.   But we nurse doubts and fears,
Ape, shuffle, cringe, the dapperlings of life,
Feed whimsy with a spoon, drink deep of foam,
Efts in the morning, deified at eve.
I half incline to Arthur and his text.
'T is life we seek, perennial, native, free,
That circulates in action, drains the world
To the lees and flings the empty goblet by.
These cogitations craze the blood and spring,
Harvests of dragon-teeth, a fiery host
Full-armed for onset."
                              " Heigh-ho," said the Smith
     " Is wisdom bitter to her darlings?   Nay.
Somewhat's awry.   Albeit no weanling I

Of hers, nor from her Amazonian paps
Ever drew substance. Better thus, mayhap.
Your chin is smooth as any velvet peach,
Nor time yet brushes from your cheek the dew,
What, do you feed the worm of melancholy?
Leave this to age that moans a youth misused,
Hopes darkened, shattered schemes. But you, nay,
    lad,
You hug the haven yet, your eye knows not
The sea's mid-tempest. Pish, you sulk too soon.
By Thor, at your years I sang alway, blithe
As larks at morning, blackbirds at the noon,
Or gleeful swallows wheeling down the eve.
Perchance there was a secret in it, lad,
It may be that the thing whereon I wrought
Preserved me, and the tool forever plied.
For not with silken touches have I known
The weapons of my labor. Dawn and dusk
Have heard the anvil upon which I toiled
Groan with the thunders of my fashioning,
Nor ever seen the spark upon my forge
Cease from its bickering."
                And Vivian then,
" Whoso would have the pearl must pay the price.
Not less I half preceive this fruit we pluck
Is ashes at the core, and knowledge too,
The armorial sign of fools, a perilous wisp
Tempting to Stygian fens. Sceptre or sledge,
What differs, if we strike in tune with law?
From toiling hands a purer piety
Ascends, than from the cauldrons where are brewed

The polities and systems of all time.
O doubly blest, sir, you, on whom the plagues,
That strike at such as stuff themselves with books,
Have never breathed in baleful pestilence ! "

But Ethan turned upon him sharp and said,
" I read my Bible and my Shakspeare, lad,
Heigh-ho, these two are books enough for me.
And if I chance to turn a later page,
Some leaf that Will and Allen pore upon,
It is too idle and I cast it down.
Heigh-ho, I think the time is fed on milk
All color but no pith, all whey, no curd.
I know not if I know this malady
That cankers you, nor like the Master here,
Feel I the bottom with my fathoms, lad.
Untempered I, unhewn, nor babble oft
Beyond the lessons of my craft.   But yet
I 've had a glimpse or two, have heard the ring
Of hammers that were never swung by man.
And seeing that my bones yearn to you, lad,
Heigh-ho, I 'll hang my rag of wisdom out.
Sieze then the haft of labor and forget
Past, future, world and man himself in that
You shape with fiery consecration.   So
You make a supplication unto laws,
The strong, controlling nurses of the world,
Old and impartial, whose hard breasts undrained
Will yield you marrow and full power.   My lad,
Believe me, these plain prayers are never vain.
God lives, the earth turns, sun and moon give light,

Man comes and has his season and returns.
'T is said, things were not rightly framed at first,
And that the willful sphere has snapped a beam.
If this be so, by Thor, it strikes my mind,
Not you nor I will mend it, lad. O shame,
To prate of Evil alway, quake and moan
Until the spectre curdles all our veins.
Arise, 't is but the mirage of the mind,
That flees, you marching.   And if man were man,
Were only man, not God nor archangel,
This thing were not : but he is less than man.
I let God do his work and I do mine.
I let the world roar and I hold my own.
All is not mine, but what is, that I keep ;
My life is mine to use it as I can.
Work then, my lad, strike early and strike late,
And small or great so that your deed be pure,
'T will purge like a strong wind the heart of gloom
And rout the host of profitless inquest
That blow their ram's horns round about your walls
To force them crumble.   Heigh-ho, come with me,
And hear my Will and Allen sing a rhyme
I taught them when their hands first felt the sledge."

Beside the forge they found the Anakim
Dark-haired, broad-shouldered. And at Ethan's voice
They came to greet their slender visitants
With eyes of cloudless courtesy and words
That witnessed of an inner dignity,
Of hearts self-reverent.   They lifted up
Deep voices and the alternate hammer rang.

Here is breaking a new brightness,
Rouse, and gird the soul with laughter,
Take the swiftness and the lightness,
And persistence that comes after.
  Strike, strike.
Seeds of hope within you cherish,
Let the sin and sorrow perish.

Smile when thickest wrongs oppress you,
When disasters hasten, sing.
Will you have God's love to bless you,
Find that love in everything.
  Strike, strike.
Lift the thought and purge the passion,
Upward change for aye in fashion.

Nought is lacking, menials myriad
Watch your steps with fond devotion,
Stars of fate are rolled in period,
Round you with melodious motion.
  Strike, strike.
Fullest life the heavens bequeath you,
Plant the stable world beneath you.

Aye achieving, aye resigning,
Life be simple, life be holy.
Teaching, founding, not repining,
Take the perfect stature slowly.
  Strike, strike.
Nearest hest is clearest duty,
Purest heart the surest beauty.

So much the noble Smith and his bold sons
Took hold on them, they tarried till the eve
Perched in the elm above them, then set forth
Reluctantly, with promise to explore
Again the genial nook.   And as they moved,
The eve, descending from her sapphire heights,
Through labyrinthine purples disappeared,
With many a fond delay and backward glance ;
And from the heart of twilight slowly rose
The diamond fabric of the night, complete
In splendor round its everlasting dome.

V.

NOBLE forever the man
Who builds his life serenely,
Divine in scope and plan ;
Droops not his eye, but keenly
Pursues a law sublime and sure,
A law of beauty that will endure,
Of melody that is sweet and pure,
Which beam and rafter will hear with glee
And silently fall into harmony.

He is master of the shield,
He is cunning with the spear,
Never warrior rode afield,
So swift and sure and clear.

Cold as sunlight upon snow,
Warm as summer in her passion,
Veering to strange winds that blow
Never in the selfsame fashion,
Changeling of each passing spell,
What he was could few men tell,
Albeit the greatness of his soul
Slumbered peaceful as the pole
Round which a hundred planets roll.

It will guide him and inform,
Though every star be lost in storm,
And what it does forbid or bid,
He shuns or seeks with glee,
And nothing from his mind is hid,
That known to it should be.

Foes approach in threatening guise,
He steals their weapons, charms their eyes,
Friends with costly aid arrive,
He shows them all they hoped to give.
He knows the secret ordinance,
The impulse and the goal ;
Amid the wild and winding dance
Of shifting fate and eddying chance,
Moves the fulfilling soul,
Culling by nice affinity,
Shaping with wise dexterity,
Fusing with fiery unity,
Till on its orbit roll
A fair and starlike whole.

———◆———

The maiden Dawn yet dreamed within her bower.
The voice of Phosphor, singing nigh her couch,
Long time had stirred her crimson-veinéd lids
With gentle tremors through their silken grain,
Ere she awoke and timidly peeped out
From half-oped lattice, baring one smooth cheek,
O'er-sprinkled with the rose, to soothe awhile

The amorous throbbings of the minstrel star.
" Aside, aside, those jealous curtains sway ; "
He sang with lingering passion as he rose,
"Ye tardy Hours, will ye not loose the folds
Of silver-wefted fingering, that I
With one long glance of love may cool mine eyes ?
Hard-hearted !   For before her feet forsake
Her argent arbors, I must die forlorn
Far up in heaven."   But his mourning fell
Fainter and ever fainter till the Morn
Entered his chariot-shell.   His bright steeds shook
From their white manes the foamy hyaline,
And drove the golden surf round cloudy isles,
Mooring at last by purple-breasted shores
Rimming the west.   And here he disembarked
And moved supreme, his ray-embroidered vest
Floating on gentle winds from loosened bands
As with imperial glance he turned to eye
His wide celestial realm.
                    Upon the bench
Before his cottage-door the Master mused :
" Name ye it death because the soul is blending
With beauty and the majesty of being?
Behold, his glorious head from darkness freed,
Grandly the peaks of light his wheels ascend,
Fraught with a holy purpose, a desire
Amplest and loftiest.   Ah, Heosphor, now
The large fair smiles are fading from thy face,
And while round saffron cliffs thy chariot bends,
The luminous surges shatter at thy back.
Not sad art thou.   With thee 't is calm and well,

Albeit thy sweetness grows invisible,
Whelmed in the ocean of a mightier light.
Not death, not death : but unto life more clear,
Higher and heavenly great our paths belong."

Sounding the close, his voice swelled like a trump,
And from their pillows drew the Three, who dozed
In wigwams wattled of the plundered pine.
And each in matin welcome kissed the brow
They reverenced above the front of kings.
"To-day the Lake is ours," said Vivian, "come,
Not yet the rose is opened on her stem,
The bee not ventures ; 't is the sweetest hour ;
Come, let us smell the Morning in her bud."
And Paul made up a roll of sandwiches,
And dipping cheerily from hill to vale,
They took for guide a froward brook that drew
Tremulous trails of shining waves through deep
Ravines, and darting tauntingly before,
Chided their lagging feet with summoning shouts.
And by the pebbly shallows leaping wild,
The younger travelers tingled all the air
With merriment ; shot random shafts of wit,
Frolic discourse aglow in every word
From happy pulses, lavish of their fire.
Profuse in praise of every charm they met,
These for a season loosed the rigid rules
That gird us in the daily course of life,
Forgot the pressing future and its needs,
Forgot the secret cares that baffle hope,
Forgot grave puzzles in the thread of life,

Half taught that all was pastime or a dream.
Treading the long-ribbed margin where the lake
Swam in repose, robbed of her central pulse,
The Three doffed vestment and embraced the flood,
Breasting the willing waves.   And flushed anon
With easy mastery, put boldly forth
To buffet with the lordliest surge they found ;
But soon with panting sides and aching arms
Set foot on shore and welcomed boot and coat.

And thus renewed, like sons of Jove they clomb
A jutting bank and on the woven moss
That sloped through cedarn boughs, sat down and
        watched
The great lake widen and the sky come down,
The shadowy bars that reached from shore to shore,
White ships that turned to vassal wind and wave,
Half-buried in the distant west or clear
From figure-head to mizen-top.   A shore
Abrupt curved slowly southward and shook out
High beads of oak and pine above the seas.
Northward far-off a rim of half-guessed land
Plunged like a sword into the golden west.
Beneath, the meek waves wooed the stubborn rock
Flinging a dolorous murmur round its brows,
And ever ceased not from their suppliant task,
Urged by a power unrespited, more stern
Than the brute tyrant whom they ran to kiss.

And having seen and heard, they turned the page
Of one who sang his honied thought divine

Sweeter than Lydian air or Phrygian lute,
Yet sometimes rugged as the hymning seas ;
Beloved, him who wears the faultless leaf.
Whereon a magic languor seized their souls,
And airy-footed Silence came and pressed
Large draughts of visioned nectar to their lips.
And they, spell-stricken as before a God,
Drank, and fell deeper into mystic dreams,
Lost sense of lake and sky and ship and shore,
Wide-wandering through low-bosomed lands that
    breathed
With delicate music swaying round and round ;
Beheld things new and wondrous, gods and men
Mixt ; and lofty summits lustrous-dim
With purple light ; and heard the syren chat
Of viewless nymphs with silvery laughs and sighs.
Thus the swift trances came and broke and blended,
Soothing, beguiling them of conscious thought,
Until a coarse cry, grumbled from a skiff,
Oared noisily by early fishermen
Bringing the spoil from newly-lightened nets,
Thrust ruinously up its presence there
Amid the misty splendor of their sleep.
And as a Nereid bevy tremulous,
Just startled by the footing of a man,
Dive with low shrieks into their coral halls,
So these weird fancies fled them, and they waked
Uncertain and bewildered in the shade.

The Patriarch smiled at them, and partly shamed
That such effeminate sorcery had wiled

The sternness from their bosoms, stolen so deft
The keys that do unlock the castled calm
Of manhood, and possessed their gates and towers,
They snatched a fairy tome of Greek, and read
How Epictetus taught the Roman world
To build their lives of stately mould, of strength
Rock-hewn from granite or the Parian stone.
And having tasted of the Stoic fount,
Their hearts won back their firmness, and all shame
Fled like a vapor from the polar chill.

A boat drew nigh.   They hired it and embarked.
And Vivian sought the poop, but Paul gave out
The snowy bosom of a minion sail
To the cool breeze ; and Arthur sat astern,
Playing upon the rudder with a palm
Perfect in pilotage, that thrilled the bark
With every veering impulse of his will ;
Obedient to the spirit of his touch
As a love-breathing lute unto the quick
Warm fancies of a maid in wooing-time.
An hour the keel spun forth the silver wake,
An hour, in front, burgeoned a breadth of seas.
Then from the wave a baby isle was born,
Wearing upon its brow what seemed a star
Or crag-caught meteor, smit with fiery throes
Till it resume its heaven and unfold
Its error wild.   They moored beside a strand,
Pied with bright pebbles, smooth as those calm
        banks
Where Triton wont to lead his ocean-bands,

And blow his horn through all a summer's day.
Atlantis in her dawn of loveliness,
Nor gardens of divine Alcinoüs,
Nor those impurpled meads whose fabled bloom
Cushioned the feet of the immortal race,
Surpassed this fair demesne.   To them it seemed
All seasons breathed an equal influence,
Perpetual music floated from the bowers,
And that all skies were fortunate as where
The prime ancestor held discourse with Heaven
In his supremest hour.   Lush champaign lawns
Bubbled in founts that veiled their naiad eyes
With leafy lids or gushed from snowy urns
Where sea-gods dreamed in marble.   There were
        groves
Luxurious and lined with silky gales ;
Boughs of all leaves, from which fine odors rain
Like fainting melodies, in whose thick shades
Dian drew back the arrow to its head,
Or white-armed Danaid spilled the pattering wave.
All round a harmony of rills ; all round
Clear pearls of sound, the largess of all throats.
Midmost, an isle within the isle arose,
In cone ascending to its summit, crowned
With a white fabric builded temple-wise,
Whose burnished dome flashed crystal in the sun.
And round the inner isle a silent stream,
In perfect circle ordered, moving, seemed
Like Saturn's silver ring that without sound
Wheels on its orb with steps severe and slow.
From this went radiations of bright rills

Outward in stairs of cataract to the lake,
Building the iris of purpureal beams ;
Melodious in their purl as those which lulled
The drowsy Heroes lapt in asphodel.
All seemed the shadow of a high intent,
The poesy of some mysterious dream ;
As if a bold magician, vision-struck,
Lured by ideäl glimpses in his soul,
Had given to enchanted thoughts investiture
By fine creative charm cunningly said.

"A myth, a myth," cried Vivian. "Paul, 't is yours,
Whose fancies swarm like golden atomies
On a slant sun-beam, to devise conceit
Or legend rhyming with the spot." And Paul,
"Come, sit by Nilus and his sphinx, and hear.
I 'll feign a baby poet, fair as morn,
Under Arcadian awnings fast asleep.
Up from the sea a hoary mariner,
As old as Hindus fable of their priests,
Appears, and spying the pellucid pearl,
Hides it within his bosom and embarks.
Past cape and port, from ocean-belt to belt,
His wreathen steeds, from deep Neptunian stalls
Fresh-yoked, and shaking starlight from their manes,
A day and night spurn back the liquid leas.
By this fair isle his beak of crystalline
He bridles, and upon the sumptuous sward
Places the slumber-sanguined child in shade
Of a paused cloud that brims with orange hues.
Angels he summons ministrant, calls up

Ambrosial influences that shall guide
His feet where fruits immortal ripen, where
Eternal fountains flow.   He tasks the suns
With their most gracious energies to weave
Gently into his lucent cheek the soft
And vermeil dartings of auroral skies,
And in his eyes the light of beauty lodge.
Shielded by wisdom and by triple love,
Thus would the essential young divinity
Rejoice with secret gladness.   Here no voice
Of a sad world in agony would mar
Imaginative soarings.   Governance
That nips the fancy in its virgin grace
Or trips the instinctive pacings of the mind,
Nor falsity profaning the young thought,
Would cloud the heavenly orbing of his soul,
Nor league his spotless hands with infamy.
But this great seer should set to golden laws
The tumult of his youthful harmony
And teach his will a wise celerity.
And when his heart was perfect and his mind
A brightness, he should cleave the backward foam
And bring a new Saturnian age to men."
But Arthur's mocking laugh rang loud and sure
As thunder after levin, and he said,
"O dainty bard, O most miraculous bard !
He 'd write his songs in mystic runes, I guess,
On earth unfathomable.   I fancy him,
Serenely sailing, on a sudden struck
Through all his sails by fiercest critic flaws,
His spars plucked like a goose, and all his bright

Streamers wide-winnowed round the skies.   **O pish!**
I am no vates, but meseems the Seer
Should centred stand in his humanity,
Interpreting the time unto itself.
Is poesy the froth of idle wits,
The flaunting of a false and painted plume?
May moping dreamers wanton with her locks,
Or fools play suitor to her shining limbs?
The hoiden bard whose leprous hands assoil
Her vestal snow, and seek to drag her down
Through miry marts to mate with courtesans,
Scarce wanders from his office more than he
Who always strikes his lyre in apogee.
But this pink-fancied gentleman you paint
Were better of a wassail bout or two.
O dainty bard, O perfect bard, O bard!"

And Paul, "Nay, you are harder than a stone,
Passing the worth and thundering on the fault.
For all is dream, or most.   I only seek
The dream within the dream."   But Arthur cried,
"Behold, I starve upon your idle stuff.
Fetch forth the sandwiches and let us eat."
And while they broke their fast and drank the urn
Of Nilus, in a neighboring grove arose
A clear and trilling laughter uncontrolled,
Whose music played upon the island-hush,
Touching the keys of silence till she sang
A song of silver echoes right and left.
Then all was still as long a time as glides
Betwixt two pipings of a perchéd lark.

And while the Three stared round with troubled eyes,
Jaws pausing at their tasks and crusts half raised,
Peal followed ringing peal, like parleying horns
In merry England when the fox is up.
Rising, they caught through leafy bosks the flash
Of ivory necks and snowy-fluttering folds.
And one, who seemed the queenliest, came and said,
Her cheeks all crimson, "Pardon us, we pray.
It was our hap, not choice.   Before we saw,
We heard.   We beg you, take not from our mirth
An alien sense of pain."   She turned to fly.
"Ah, Cora," said the Sire, "you know me not?"
But at his voice she came and took his hands
And bade him welcome, welcome.   "Sir, I'm sure
Your heart will overlook it.   I saw not,
So giddy with my strange discourteous plight.
'T is long since you have come.   How old you seem!
Daily my father names you.   We have planned
Some day to clamber to your hermitage."
She called her troop of maidens, lovely nymphs,
Eyes of all iris, golden brows and dark,
Cheeks rosed or lilied, dimpled or sedate,
Pink lips and pearly teeth and milky palms.
All mingled straight in cordial intercourse
Until the Master drew his youth away
To seek the host within the inner isle.
Crossing the flood on fairy arcs of wire,
That mimicked, with apt shape and color, spans
Of rainbow, thence they clomb with loitering looks
From flowery terrace unto terrace up.
The Host came forth and greeted them; a man

Ripe in an eye that drank the world like light.
Faint furrowy traces meted out his brow,
Foot-prints of oft-alighting thought ; his cheeks,
Ruddy and lightly touched with wisest lines,
Swept down in stately curve upon a chin
Majestic, calm, whereon all storms were wrecked.
Through marble columns passing in, they found
Ample saloons and hung with gorgeous folds,
Product of cunningest looms ; as rare, perchance,
In texture as the wondrous tissues wrought
By young Arachne ; emblem and device
Embroidered, pointing to a secret sense,
Yet manifold in type and tint to please
Fastidious eyes.   And everywhere were nooks
Monastic, shy recesses girt with tomes ;
The Delphic utterance of all time.   Long halls
He opened.   And whate'er the soul of man
With impulse bold has wrested from the scope
Of lawless nature by victorious thought,
Was there incarnate in divinest form,
Perfect unto his hope.   And one contained
Choicest and sweetest forms of harmony,
In which the burning heart aspires to pour
The passion of its mortal ecstacy,
Its proud expectancy and lofty cheer,
The height of its desire.   All instruments
Of softest chord or finest-ordered reed
Tempted the skillful hand, and in the midst
Polymnia touched the lyre with eyes that drew
Their melodies from heaven.   And one was shown,
Thick-peopled with those manly brows august,

Who fought and overcame, simple and brave,
Not scorning to be just, through loss and harm
Loyal to holy aims, entire of blame.
And one unfolded on its pictured walls
Methods of piety, whereby the soul,
Suppliant, seeks divine deliverance
From earthly thralls, an immortality.

And these were ranged concentric to the dome,
That rained perpetual splendor like to that
Beheld with wildered eyes upon the top
Of Paradise by the dazed Florentine.
Centre of all, of temple and of isle,
Behold, alighting on a golden sphere,
A burning seraph glowed, her wings just furled
From some divine career.   The snowy vans
Were dyed with vermeil flushes, and her lips
Stirred with a smile of utter sweetness, calm
And holy to inspire the soul that gazed
With saintly passion.   On the sphere was writ,
" Beauty has golden ordinance of her own.
Her feet in one unchanging cycle move.
Ever unto herself a sphere complete,
She must repeat herself unto herself
By an eternal love."   Some hours The Three
Strolled with increasing wonder and delight
The enchanted palace, while the elder twain
Discoursed without in pleasant shade, alone.
On plinth and pedestal, cornice and frieze
They read a hundred mottoes sown in gold,
Bright as the finger that aforetime scared

The Babylonite ; deep precepts that contained
The pith of stateliest wisdom old and new,
All centering upon culture and how best
The soul may touch its greatest. Weighed with lore,
Like argosies from Ind, they left the halls,
And sought the Masters, mingling word of thanks
With lavish eulogies.   And Vivian said,
" I solve not the full meaning, but all seems
To meet in Beauty, the Ideäl one."

" This is my chosen covert from the glare
Of summer," said the Host, " a prank of years
Untempered, that into exhaustless mines
Of fortune dropped a hand too prodigal.
I have enforced the islet to express
The visual symbol of a phantasy
That shaped the meditations of those days.
Ever the law of culture wrought in me ;
Without, a discord, but within, a peace.
I saw brave spirits crushed beneath the weight
Of their own selves, enduring energies
Canceled by trivial bias or misuse,
A thousand battle and one wear the crown.
And I perceived a law behind the world
That came and overcame, but made its home
In man, and in the inly-motioned mind ;
Mine and not thine, or thine not mine, a law
Of personality, which gave and took,
Knew to accept and to reject by choice
Instinctive, and I wrought from hour to hour
Wisely to amplify this mastership.

For from the primal hands which have assigned
Its own elliptic unto every star,
The many-ordered soul of man receives
Some impulse of peculiar destiny,
His own, and which he may not e'er forego.
Herein is hid the reason and the height
Of his attainment.   Centred upon this,
He gently radiates his million beams,
Drinking the dew from the celestial flower,
Beauty, the truest amaranth, and adds
His harmony unto the noble choir,
The universal anthem that ascends
From a victorious humanity.
Then, on all peaks a light of God ; within,
Olympian power to purpose and achieve."

And Vivian, " Culture, culture, 't is a word
Noised in my ears by every hand that clangs
The philosophic cymbals.   Does it bear
A weightier meaning than our fathers knew ?
Is it not heartless?   Can its veins take fire
With any liberal self-renouncing hope ?
Grant it a majesty, 't is cold and stern
As Alpine glaciers, crushing as they move."

And with a smile the Host made answer calm.
" There needs the equal hand that drew of old
The circle, to configure her in full,
The imperial Art, to which all meaner use
Brings hostage ; her domain the permanent soul,
Its proud ascensions, majesty of doom,

Nor less the world, its ages, races, deeds,
Sins, sorrows, wisdoms, mounting pieties;
Her method life, mysterious interchange
Of each with each, fine unison of laws
Receptive and creative.   Man and world,
Urim and Thummim on her bosom shine.
I trust not unto flighty aims that skim
Sublimely all the heavens, but mostly miss
The occasion that implores a remedy.
Nor much avails who, couched on learned down,
Prates all day long of an ideäl world;
Less he, who bondaged unto sensuous tasks,
The inglorious menial of himself, kneads bricks
In Egypt, never purging from his soul
The hideous grime, nor lifting heavenward gaze
To pierce the sooty vapors of his kiln.
But life is mediator 'twixt two worlds,
Reäl, ideäl; unto neither given,
But fusing both into a throbbing whole,
The possible present.   All is use, but man,
Ever the master-user, uses use.
Thence are there wise eclectic arts that pluck
Its proper excellence from every thing:
Souls that with cunning sympathies endued,
Read secrets where none seem, unsymbolize
Material forms, perceive a wondrous light
Set in the heart of midnight, or descry
A darkness blazoned on the front of noon.
For not in fiery gazing vision lies,
But in the cunning couching of the eye.
There are, of their own hearts incontinent,

Weak prodigals of their best attribute,
Who alienate high heaven by suits ill-timed.
Await, if your expectancy be void,
Weep not, the loss will hatch a golden gain."

And Vivian said, " This lesson gives me joy.
Instructed, by the Master, of the Soul,
Scorn darkened in me for a world debased ;
Content and grateful to behold no more
Her sodden lineaments, nor ever hear
The surge and welter of her panic seas.
Nobler Stylites or far Therapeut
Riddling the law symbolic in his shrine,
Or Brahmin, visioned child of loneliness,
On large conitions elevate to blend
With Vishnu, inexhaustible, supreme.
Yet hour by hour with looks of keen reproach
She came before me, and a pang was born
That aught by God created should be held
Unclean and an abhorrence. And this law
Of a benign alliance which you name,
Of world with man, proud uses of the soul,
Is dear to me. O lift yet more the veil."

And the Host said, " Strive not to strive amiss.
O rail not at the world, nor scorn, but use ;
How, none may teach you but yourself alone.
Prelude to this august election, purge
The eyes of film, the breast of mortal fear,
And make desire in lustral fountains white ;
Lead then the spirit up the fulgent sides

Of the mount of God, into the awful cloud
Have entrance, and with face low-bowed await
Prescript celestial.   From this hour no more
Your goings in and out belong to you.
A sign will move before you, and a voice
Haunt you with high behest.   Thence you will live
By the one law, your own, not less nor yet
Greater; unto yourself will be an aim,
A fullness and a beauty, and advance
Thereby the full behoof of humankind.
Calm will your days succeed, not tossed and wrecked
By myriad askings of the double world,
Within, without.   Rejecting all that works
Discord into the music of your thought,
Content to bear, forbear, equal to seek
The One through guises of the Manifold,
Your heart shall be instinct with light, itself
Within itself complete, not asking help.

" O for some fine and airy syllable,   ·
To prison in one perfect sound the soul
Of this high theme !   Medea's cauldron she,
From which the lifeless fragments of the world
Come forth a living creature fair and young;
Darkness and light, nadir and zenith met ;
The one, the all ; atom and universe ;
The protean elf of utter paradox.
What eye discerns in subtile rise and fall
The fairy lungs of the rose, or from the bee
Lures his deft takings-up and passings-by ?
Culture is all.   Ever the larger eye,

The purer heart.   The sphere her symbol is.
She shuns not, nor disdains, nor is too fond.
Sunlike her beams brood over sea and marsh,
Thence plucking exhalations that will feed
Her chosen plots, her nooks of Paradise.
She lays the axe upon the crumbling roots
Of old authority, and on her front
Wears ' Freedom ' graven as her sole device,
Freedom, word used by all, by most misused,
Freedom, by all men claimed, by few achieved,
A few great hearts who hand her down to us.
The earth at first a centric core of flame,
Floated for ages round the nebulous pools.
Then rained the slime, spawned monsters, and at last,
Flourished the climes and seasons, and the earth
Rolled through her sister-lights a perfect star.
Slowly the cycles finish : let us wait.
Go, play like children in the light of beauty
And so be safe.   Love well what is your own,
And Love will make the universe your own.

" Inspired by reason, we reclaim the soul,
Point after point of gnarled wilderness
Subdued by lavish spending of our strength,
From states of nature, till a land ensue
Waving with plenteous harvests.   Thus we come
To know the highest purport of this art
Which consummates the features of the mind ;
The universal axis on which she
With all her stately constellations turns.
And this is Beauty, the original Form.

Poising on subtle scales the circumstance,
She tempers life with fitting ordinance,
The outer and the inner world adjusts
Musically each to each. She guides, impels,
Spurs, curbs ; ever subjecting word and deed
To the law. She fuses day in day and melts
The iron years to mould her high intent.
Her plastic hands endue humanity
With clear immortal graces. She informs
With unity the broken ore of life.
Unresting she perfects her handiwork,
Imbreathes her burning ideäl in man,
And incarnates her godhood, meting forth
With a fine insight, exquisitest skill,
Faint finger-throes of finish, till at last
Beauty, supreme and in eternal calm,
Stands sole, and yields delight to heaven and earth.

" But who shall lift the fancy beyond this?
What tongue shall sing of Beauty ? Who shall prove
Her Godhead ? For she dwells too high, too far
For vision, deep-sequestered in the heart
Of that unchanging Soul whom we adore.
Does true divinity to mortal eye
Disrobe herself? Contented we discern
Some polished shoulder-tip or ankle-curve
Imperial, or mysterious roseate glow
Ambushed amid the many-folded vest,
Stirred by some earthly lover's amorous palm,
Who would discover the celestial features.
Ah, evermore content must we remain

With golden glimpses, stifling so the pangs
Of fruitless longings.   Patience yet a while.
She will abide and we will mount to her.
Hers are the final laws of things.   Strong **Truth**
His master-sickle swings and binds his sheaves
To bring to her the princely revenue.
Mild virtue plants her gardens with sweet loves,
To weave for her a chaplet.   Poet, priest
And prophet, lordliest of the mortal throng,
Are sons of her infinity and draw
From her their holiness.   The moons and stars,
Broad-flowing in eternal streams of light,
The fair earth with her million forces, all
That seems or is, subserves her cosmic will
And shadows forth the meaning of her soul.
And hand in hand appears beside her, Love."

They listened with due reverence.   Then he rose
To lead them through the Isle, and while they walked,
All shared the conversation.   They discussed
The lofty Eld when men appeared as Gods,
Or paused in rapture where those spirits trod, —
Drunk from the honey-lip of him whose voice,
Swelled in perpetual warble through the grove, —
The shadowy sward beside Illissus, heard
The golden discourse, saw the godlike brows;
Or mounted with the wrinkled sage who thought
Beside the Baltic, or that bolder man,
His worthy son and full co-heir of thought,
World-proof, and equal to his daring creed;
Or with the imperial Eye of Weimar saw

The world dissolving type by type ; beheld
Milton hold firm his seraph gaze to catch
The ineffable in white mid-splendor ; or
Shakspeare fling all the portals wide of that
Serene majestic palace of his soul,
While the great world surged through in audience.
And as they moved fresh wonders of the place
Leaped into view and won their passing praise ;
Delphos, Dodona, cave and temple wrought
In miniature ; a whorl of labyrinth ;
Villa or school or grot of hermitage,
Stoa or Tusculun or Academe ;
Conceits and schemes of fancy, rare and quaint.
But one lone dell most charmed them where a doe
Browsed with her fawns, and high above them towered
A mighty stag and watched the visitors,
Antler flung high and bold eye unabashed.
And at the master's call he came and ate
The herbage from his hand and leaned his head
Across his shoulder, careless of the rest.
Thence skirting a thick grove they spied the form
Of Cora perched upon a pedestal
From which a Nymph had fallen. Wide she swung
White arms of oratoric emphasis
Above the bevy, mute in audience.
And somewhat thus her scornful treble rang.
" Trust not the easy and Ulyssean tongue,
Although his incense sweeter rise than myrrh,
Who would yoke Love to Beauty to upturn
Furrows of Mammon, blushing not to sell
Wisdom, that should be holy, and the sense

Of noble speech to basest uses.   Nay,
But let us seize the Reäl and stand firm.
We marry not the acre nor the purse,
But something that will help our lives to be
An ampler beauty.   And the canticles
Of Love, sole-sung in pianissimo,
More charm, than with a basso like a frog."

They laughed and clapped their tiny hands and
        laughed :
They trilled a sweet " Bravissima," and laughed ;
And those who overheard caught up the cry,
And pealed a loud " Bravissima," and laughed,
Till half the Isle, quaffing the quick delight,
Laughed tipsily in bosk and bank and dell.
" I beg your pardon, Cora," said her Sire.
" You play the demagogue with grace.   The part
Flows from you smoothly ; you are schooled in it.
A year of Burke, some random hours to catch
The trick of fulsome Ciceronian ease,
And you are faultless.   But change first your theme.
This shakes the nerves of manly anditors,
Breathing sedition."   Then her burning cheek
Pleaded for pity, and his heart was moved
In Arthur.   " Rather let me hear," he said,
" Faction herself let loose, if she but couch
In such sweet tones her argument, than all
The homilies of duteous loyalty."
Whereat the warring chiefs flung down their arms,
And laughed and gave the reconciling kiss.
They talked and jested of the tables turned,

And played at shuttlecock with harmless wit,
Moving to lunch in arbors by the beech,
Where ample vases piled with golden fruit
Tempted the eye.   And all day long they woo'd
Fleet pleasures, ever varied, ever sweet.
The maidens touched guitar in grove or bower,
Or warbled dainty staves of chosen songs,
Or, grouped in snowy band in the great Hall,
Blended the tones of diverse instruments,
Lifting in charming choir more stately rhythms,
Verdi, Bellini, Beethoven, Mozart;
Or rocked in cushioned gondolas that swayed
Voluptuously from flowery bank to bank,
They moved upon the soft translucent flood
In shady circles, touched at fragrant ports,
And boasted to have sailed around the world.
At eve they parted, planning joys to come.
But Arthur dallied with the helm, and while
His vessel lingered nigh the shore, he sang:

> Smile the gods, but smile benignly
> When through life's unfolding portal
> Ruddy from the morn above,
> Boldly rush twin spirits mortal,
> Meet and mingle all divinely,
> Breathed upon by Love.
>
> Smile the gods, but not in scorn.
> For they burnish with new splendor
> The bright axle of the morn.
> Magic charms, illusions tender

Then they lavish, and the Graces
Summon from their secret places,
Cunning-handed aid to render.

With enchanted purple lining
All the chambers of the world,
Lo, upon the air unfurled,
Lustrous folds of light are shining.
All the vales are paved with brightness,
Every rose is dew-impearled,
And the lark's song floats for lightness.

And these twain are mute with feeling,
Hand to hand and lip to lip,
While a golden fire is stealing
Forth through every finger-tip.
And young Love, whose heavenly nature
Is compact of harmony,
So transforms their mortal feature
That each seems to either eye
Some divine immortal creature.

Slowly cease the lips from kisses,
Slowly droop the burning glances,
Slowly fade the rosy blisses,
Slowly break the mystic trances ;
Gently toward their passion warm
Comes the step of destiny,
Gently round each trembling form
Steals the stern and fateful arm,
Till they part to meet no more,

And between them flows a sea
Without ship or shore.

Smile the gods, but graciously.
This was thus by their decree.
For the dream they dreamed was surer
Than our waking thoughts may be,
And the sweetness made them purer
And the agony.

Closing, they greeted him with plausive cheer
And gesture, while the skiff sprang lightly forth
To a quick wind, and all through half a league
The fluttering kerchief shook from boat and shore
A thousand sweetly lingering, sad farewells.
Then Arthur's hand slept on the helm ; it seemed
Something was left behind him in the Isle.
And Paul leaned back upon the prow and watched
The glassy forehead of the westward lake
Put on its fiery turban, till he said,
" Listen ; for while we clove the little belt
Of waters and the voice of Cora lulled
So dreamily the fancy, a strange hand
Was laid upon me by the Happy Isle,
Its loneness and its gladness, and I saw,
Or seemed to see, the blissful Heroes go
And come among the shadows, and I heard,
Or seemed to hear, mild and enlarged words,
Serenest utterance of reposing souls.
Slowly the discourse gathered up to one,
Where nigh the bank Achilles with his friend,

Patroclus, talked.   And what he seemed to say
I will repeat to lend our voyage wings."
And with soul-touching cadences he sang.

"Shot hither from the sounding bow of time,
We rust not idly upon barren sands,
But have become a greater, as we know,
Purged of the grosser principles that wrought
Aforetime unto discord, and assigned
Unto a clearer sunlight and an air
Cleansed of those stains.   Patroclus, are we less,
In that we are not stirred by thoughts of war,
Entire of the oppressive turbulence
Native unto that ether, but from this
Forever alien?   Though 't is true it urged
To more of action there and taught the arm
Ampler achievement, thereby close allied
With mortal glory, this declares it false,
That it has fallen from us and not dared
Enter with us this region where we move
Upon harmonious paths and unto ends
Serene.   For as these purple vales outshine
That loveliest Ida, this crystalline stream
Simois, and these blessed meads Troy plain,
Bruised with the tempest of a thousand hooves,
No less Achilles in the Happy Isle
Exceeds that other of the shield and spear.
Another music we have heard, our feet
Unto a nobler pæan are advanced.
Now Hector's hand is careless of the sword,
No more Ulysses finds it sweet to roam,

And to a sceptre higher than his own
The great Atrides lifts his kingly hand.
Here is repose : not vacant of the stress
Of noble ardors, yet inviolate
By the hard clamor that confused our minds.
Yea, this endeavor, having for its scope
Wisdom and Beauty in full amplitude,
Differs from that as the firm-ordered march
Of manhood from uncertain infancy.
They wander in the world of-shades, not we.
All the hand compassed or the eye beheld
Were broken shadows of this mighty world
We now inhabit.   There the race of men
Pursue alway fleet-footed fantasies
That lure them into perilous straits, albeit
'T is theirs to draw from weakness and mischance
The wondrous sustenance that makes them Gods.
O friend, whose dearness taught me to put by
My low abasement and resume the weight
Of that intent, from which too long divorced
My heart was cankered on the idle deck,
Though we were mortal, we are grown divine,
Nor can remembrance of our cloudy prime
Eclipse these stately splendors, nor abate
The perfect sweetness of this golden clime.
From the great Gods our state is less removed.
No longer shod with terror and dismay,
As when they mingled with the files of men,
Their awful sandals glimmer as they come.
But now, invested with a gentle grace
Of brotherhood, they touch upon our sphere,

And walk beside us through the blissful shades
In lofty converse and majestic league,
Lavish of that large knowledge which they have,
The birth and ordinance of all that is.
But hush, Patroclus, let us not forget.
Not all ignoble was our mortal hour,
Nor all unworthy to be mused upon
Within the precincts of our blessed isle.
Was it not great to hurl the gleaming spear,
While the earth trembled to the wheels of fire,
Amid the thunders of the jarring hosts?
And not less great, sole-standing on the plain,
To watch the fiery light of Hector's eye,
And front his bold heroic enmity.
Lo, this is greater, ever with the foot
Steadfast in arduous ways, neither to pause
Nor falter, but to round the perfect sphere
Of all our attribute.   Rise, let us thread
These flowery alleys to the echoing sea,
And standing close beside its shining marge,
Behold the million motions of its feet
And hear the pleasing discord of its winds ;
There without sorrow, having what we have,
Remember all the distant world of men,
From which we have been lifted many an age,
Whose shores our wandering feet will press no more."

Long time in deepest hush they sailed, so much
The chanted pathos of his voice intense
Subdued, so long his solemn periods
Murmured from soul to soul.   And Vivian, moved

Part by the strain, but most by his own heart,
Felt a great cloud of sadness shadow him.
Musing on that resplendent Form that crowned
The golden sphere, and on her smile so sweet,
So heavenly sweet, his burning spirit yearned
For one immortal kiss from those pure lips.
And gazing long into the heavens he said,
"Dwell not too high, O spirit, in your skies ;
Woo not alway the vestal lids that wink
Upon the silver margin of the air,
Nor yet the holy calm of Hesper's eye.
At morn I saw you on the orient brink
Bathing amid the surf of golden seas ;
All day you hid in links of fleecy mail,
The armor of the mild, blue-bosomed day ;
O then come now beneath the purple zone,
That sunders earth from heaven, and meet me here.
Oped are the gateways of beseeching eyes.
Come down ; come in ; and flush with ruddy beams
My heart through all its chambers." And he paused
From a too brimming heart, then sadly sang ;

Behold, she comes from the myrtle land,
Slowly floating through evening roses,
The light of her smile serene and bland,
Like a star, fresh-blown and young, reposes ;
And before, the blossoming heavens expand,
And behind, the cloven splendor closes.

Ever and ever she floats to me,
Under the starlight, under the moon ;

My heart is high with ecstacy,
It beats, ' I will die with her soon ; '
And the skies are shaken with melody,
And the stars grow pale in a swoon.

— I care not if it be death or not,
For my heart is cold in its place,
Since she, ah God, since she forgot,
To wear the smile on her face ;
The day will be sunless, the night a blot,
Till she send me some token of grace.

" So sad ? " said Paul. " I hoped the honied chat
And tender eyes had been a passing Lethe."
" My son," the Master said, " the happier hour
Waves o'er you hands of blessing, though unseen.
Fail not in courage. Never was it known
That any soul of man intensely yearned
For Beauty and acquaintance with the Light,
And God denied it him."
                              The end was nigh.
The waters moaned. The glooming cliff flung out
A reef of darkness, and the swelling wind
Drew deeper lamentations from the pines,
That wailed like sad Cassandra, from her tower
Looking at midnight out to Samothrace,
Thinking of the dark ruin that would come.
They disembarked, and looking backward, saw,
Across the silver borders of the eve,
The battle-clouds move up in frowning ranks
To the loud bugle of the western wind ;

Pennon and plume touched with a dusky glare
Of combat.   And the Lake cast up a cry
Of fierce defiance, shook her myriad crests
In sullen foam, blew far and wide the trump
Of battle, summoning all her hosts to arms.

VI.

Central axis, pole of pole,
Central orb and goal of goal,
Worship, to whose sovereign end
All the spirit's uses tend.
Taught of her high mystery,
Perfect will the manchild be.
Not with sorrow, not with moan
Comes the soul unto her own;
Not with sounding steps of thunder,
Not with flaming looks of fire,
But with calm delight and wonder,
Simple hope and sweet desire.
Then through all the motions stealing
Of the manifold existence,
Ever lifting, soothing, healing,
Love attunes each thought and feeling
Unto patience and persistence.

And the prophet is the voice
That shall bid the world rejoice.
Youngest, eldest child of light,
Charioted on beams of morning,
Flings to the wind his banner bright,
Sounds the trump of cheer and warning.

And his swift aërial passage
Nations catch with eager eyes,
Wake the earth and shake the skies
While he speaks the holy message.
Rich his mien in charity,
Throbs his heart with ecstasy ;
His eyes are wells of mildest fire
Whence radiant issuings inspire
Deep souls with kindlings of divine desire.
Move his lips with breathings warm,
Rhythms woven of sunlight and of storm :
From God's own armory a sword
Enclothes his thigh, the flaming Word.

From wells of truth crystalline, cold,
He drinks, the passionless calm springs
That without mortal murmurings
Retain their heavenly splendors old.
Few drink ; too silken-lipped to brave
The fierceness of the unpiteous wave,
Parching with rigors manifold
Their craven souls to bondage sold,
Long used to wine in pearl and gold.
All steep and alpine loftiness,
The mountain-folds that neighboring lie
The smile of God's infinity,
He scales, to win his holiness.
And there those strong-eyed fountains glow
Whereof he gives to men below.

Half-way into a yellow afternoon
The day had slipp'd, when from his bench the Sire
Awoke from slumber, and awaking, said,
" My children, it is shown to me from heaven
That when to-morrow eve the vesper star
Shall totter on the verge of the dim world,
My spirit will be loosened from its bonds.
Once more from yonder mount would I behold
The footsteps of this Lustre.   Words I have
To utter, well befitting you to hear.
And I must lean upon you, for my limbs
Shrink from the task."   And all arose, and two
Round either neck lifted an aged arm,
And slowly and with many pauses, wound
From ledge to ledge and won a shoulder'd crest
Of plain-supporting mountain, which the sun
Smote from his place of sinking.   Here they sat
And marked the great Day vanish from his paths,
Trailing his brightness, till the western star
Opened his golden lids and shot a shaft,
Golden, of clear aërial-tempered light
That drew their gazing.   And the East, disrobed
Of all her purples, placed upon her brow
A dewy brilliant, orbing its delight
In lucid tremblings.   Overhead the stars
With timid hands unbarred their lattices,
And leaning from dark casements watched the world.
The motion and the murmur of the day
Grew slumberous in the meadows, and around
Uprose the drowsy plumes and floating down
Of Twilight, steering from her orient home.

They saw the granges nestling in the gloom,
Which deepened, and the lowing of the kine
Touched faintly on their height.   A perfect Day,
Strong, fair and wise, sank gently to his rest,
The kingly purpose of his going forth
Achieved through golden lavishment of love.
Soft-footed evening stole across the hills,
And passing, left the land with reverence still.
And all that toiled beneath the law of light,
Slept, lulled with balm from the distilling palm
Of the dim-smiling Silence, friend to all.

Then from the skies fell down an influence
Mysterious and ethereal, which crowned
The world with mystic beauty and shot awe
Into their pulses, and into their eyes
Deep love and worship ; but their lips were mute.
For either spirit was afar, beguiled
By shining thought along the happy paths
Of meditation.   Everywhere there dwelt
Upon the outer and the inner world
A wondrous wealth divine, that woke to life
The soul's supremest faculties, and dipped
The peaceful heart in a celestial dew
Of infinite love.   The essence of all forms,
The spirit of all beauty and all truth,
That which creates and moves in silence all
The powers of being, without name or form,
Divine and sole, came to them through the soul
And with them for a time abode, and they
Were speechless, motionless with holy fear.

O who would voice these golden mysteries,
Yielding unto the trumpet-clang of speech
The kissing of the human and divine !

And the age-stricken Master smiled and said,
"O when beneath the guidance of the sun
The grievous tasks are ended, and the hand
Completes its duteous offering of toil
To the inexorable Life, how sweet,
Quitting the weapons of our exercise,
While all the vales of heaven are calm with stars
And earth has smoothed the wrinkles from her face,
To slip the grosser thought and sally out
Through those eternal regions where the soul
May walk with Beauty, undeterr'd !   Alway
The mild and meditative eve inspires
Joyful devotion and refreshing hopes,
Kindles the spiritual fires anew,
Dimm'd by the light of day, and stills with **prayer**
The carking labors of the mind, that yield
Too oft a hundred-fold of pain.   All hail !
Once more, ye heavenly ministers of love,
Slow-pacing constellations, steadfast suns,
Thick-clustering signs, and willful lights that rove
Metéoric, bright cars and burning wheels
Whereon are borne the forward-sloping skies
Upon their paths eternal, but unworn !
Precious and noble is the perfect hour
Of contemplation ; and to fly the thought
Where solemn groves maintain a reverence ;
Aisles which the muffled feet of silence tread ;

Silence, the sweetest singer, taught to sweep
The grand choir-harp of God with fingers sure ;
Sweeter than fame and the wide-echoing name,
Mild nurse of purity and cheerful thoughts
Dear in themselves, spurring to arduous tasks
Wise, temperate and discerning to be just.
How gently from the hundred fading hills
And from the windings of a hundred vales
Flows the cool peacefulness in murmuring waves,
Sweeter to me than stateliest harmonies !
Love's voice falls to us from the cloud, his smile
Sits on the forehead of the rising star,
All round the margent of the shadowy world
His presence lingers.   O my children, know
That all things which for fair completion ask
Are close about you ; close about you moves
All that you may become, and from all heavens
Falls in clear smiles fulfilment of your prayers.
And what is yours seek to possess and love,
Instructed that the great gods laughingly
Sowed it through all the elements, to prove
If you deserve the larger destiny.
O not in knowledge is our end.   Her birth
Is human ; she is manifold in change ;
A heavy cloud that struggles nigh the world,
The sport of heedless gales.   She drifts and drifts.
She has to give but pangs and fears and tears,
Of that great calm we seek, incapable.
But wisdom is eternal ; from the brain
Of the Infinite her mighty being sprang.
She lodges in the soul the wondrous seed

That cannot perish, breaking into flower
Of heavenly magnificence."
   He breathed :
And they in stillness sat until he rose
And bade them lead him to a mountain tarn,
Some roods to westward. And they led him there,
And found a little pinnace moored, wherein
They entered. Then he said, " Strike oar and steer
For yonder island tufted with great pines."
And they struck oar and steered and brushed the isle
With slippery ribs, and disembarking moved
Through belts of gloom into an open cirque,
Where massy trees, ranged round in ample rings,
As if from solemn fancies, shadowed forth
A temple's nave, crowned with a dome of stars.
And the great-hearted man of many years
Gazed round him with a look of awe, and said,
" Here in my anguished hour there came to me
A heavenly vision upon wings of peace,
And perched upon my spirit like a dove."
And while the silent moments lapsed, his eye
Seemed to take root in heaven, as if his heart
Would drink to ecstasy the crystal light,
Until with lifted voice impassionate
Through all its tremor'd age he said to them ;
" We sit within the garden of the Night.
Around us sweep the harmonies of God
On viewless and inaudible wings, the flood
Of that unending hope which is our life.
Eternity is with us in the soul.
The great God in the garden speaks with us.

I hear the holy sweetness of a rhythm
Which is not of this hour, but steals far off
Along the luminous marge of other days.
Oft have I wept, fearing its voice was lost
Forever.   But to-night yon seraph star,
Touching his harp between his burning wings
Restores to me the soul of all the past.
And I become a wave among the waves
Of the melodious mystery whereof
We are a portion.   Happy is the man,
Whose soul the floods of the deep-murmuring Life
Fondle in everlasting arms.   O hour
Divine, when time lets fall her mask, and stands
Beside the hoar and old eternities,
Meek daughter!"
                    And a little space he paused;
Then turning unto Vivian said, "My son,
You have been taught of nature, man, and world,
And of the law severe.   But I, this hour,
Would name to you a mightier name than these,
Would speak of somewhat higher than all law,
Of that which cancels law and lays it by;
None other this than Love, the operant God,
Colleague of Beauty, God as immanent.
Love is the spirit of the Visible,
And works by glad surrender, lowliness;
Unselfs the self, thereby a greater self.
What hand shall teach the lyre to yield a strain
Freighted with meanings equal to the worth
Of this, the one divinest sovereign law,
The light, the glory, and the unity,

The Highest.   In the beckoning of a star,
He beckons, and when buds the folded morn,
Buds, nor the less in gloomy wombs of night
And central tides of fire, guides and impels.
By him the rose is happy and does blow,
The fearless brook slips on his dappled floors,
The belted bee buries his burnished thighs
In meadowy sweets, and the low-luting wind
Tunes the warm valley to his cooling strain.
By him the dewy lark is fed with mirth ;
By him the lone dove wanders till he finds
A cooing answering to his cooing, low
And softer than his own.   By him the stars
Have twinn'd their golden circles, and their feet
Are rich in melody.   By him all might
Makes concord with all weakness, not destroys ;
By him the One flowers to the Manifold,
By him the Manifold is but as One.
His feet are shod with music, from him flow
All subtle-pacéd harmonies that work
Through life and nature.   All the issuings,
That touch the souls of men with holy flame,
With old and simple sufferance for the True,
And warfare with enthroned forms of ill,
He feeds.   And the slow bettering of the world, —
That fond and patient creed of steadfast men, —
Is Love, self-orbing.   Throned within the soul
A king, all pulses of the active life,
All motion outward, aiming at the world,
All work, all speech, all gesture do receive
A sacred bias from his sceptre, he

With mild controlling currents tempering all
To harmonize with nature, law, and God,
To renovate, inform, expand, exalt.
He knows the canticles of Light, himself
A melody, a wisdom, a sunlight,
A beauty, a divinity, a joy,
Young, glowing, ripe, and mild and strong and fair,
One child of God, the first and latest born.

" Prophets say well that one true man saves all.
Whoso has utterly fulfilled the law,
Leaves it to all men a divine bequest.
Thus Love, who. in that God is beautiful,
Adores Him, is the Saviour of the world.
For he not hears command, nor then obeys,
Commanded, but unto himself remains
Sole origin and end, and sole delight.
Much have you heard of the individual soul,
Its singleness and its resistance, life
Self center'd.   But I bring you tidings now
Of blithe outpouring, large abandonment,
Of sacred festivals and mirth divine.
My tongue would utter that majestic hour,
The jubilee, the rapture, summing bliss,
When, all divested of its mortal husk,
The sin, the shame, the anguish cast aside,
The soul with throbs of harmony shall blend,
With all its comprehensive faculties,
With all its pathos of sublime desire,
Shall at its amplest blend with God.   O then,
Time and her shining hours fade quite away,

Space and the corporal frame of Nature flee,
And all the opacous garment of the soul
Slips into nothing, and the jarring heart,
This crackling faggot of mad contraries,
A spheric shape of tranquil flame, moves up
To the bosom of Light.   And this may come to pass
On earth, and this the babes and sucklings know.
My son, not all have stood upon this mount,
Nor any, alway; but remembrance dear
Of what it was, of what was heard and seen,
Will keep us, and to human fashionings
Extend the largess of a grace divine ;
Will rest with consecrating liberal force
Perennial, on every show of life,
Transforming into dignity and worth,
Winnowing from all endeavor what is base."

And while they sat revolving his high parle,
Slowly arose the sweetness of a voice
Soft, deep with passion tempered into joy ;
"O evening, dear because the fight is fought,
O crowning hour of hours that have been damp
With drops of wrestling, O selected hour
From all eternity, to me to bring
Celestial benediction, be thou blest,
Blessed be thou forever !   Worldly hope,
Nor lower thought than worship, shall profane
Thy glorious moments, while my days are mine."
Then Vivian told serenely and in tones
That ever gathered up the lyric force
Of a majestic spiritual hymn.

His aspect kindled from the inner heaven,
Of warfare urged through dim disastrous days,
And how the grim hostility lost ground,
He gaining, till at last he lifted up
The pæan, having won the victory.
For in this very hour, even while he heard
The Master speaking, there from heaven fell
A brightness like a falling star, and smote
His soul with blindness for a time, whereon
He was as glad and peaceful as a babe.
"And now," he said, "great Life, the manifold,
Takes on a cosmic oneness, musical,
And shapes the mazes of her thousand paths
To one sure law.   O now the world is fair,
God near, and the inspired life of man
Made fresh and true, heroic, beautiful.
O peace is ever sweet to labored men ;
The peace, that draws its sweetness from the veins
Of high fulfilment, nobly finished tasks ;
The peace, that, like a maiden, buckles on
New-forgéd armor for the wars to come."

Mildly his utterance fell upon their ears,
And blessed as a gentle summer shower.
For deeply in his spirit wrought a strength
That mellowed all his thought and every word,
And smote their minds with genial sympathy.
His bosom harbored an enduring power
Of gladness, for upon him Peace had dropped
Her robe, and Love had countervailed the world.
And over his transfigured lineaments

Lingered a bland, serene, harmonious light.
With joy the Master listened, and he raised
With travail both his aged hands and said,
" My son, I bless you for your constancy.
O peace is ever sweet to labored men.
Now is the final boon of earth to me ;
Long have I waited for this happy hour,
Solaced and 'stablished that before my death
It falls. For, Vivian, I have loved you well ;
My heart has brooded o'er you, and from you
These darkening eyes have taken half their light ;
In whom I seemed to find an echo clear
Of mine own youthful hour. And I believe
That for the witnessing of this last grace
Has Heaven deferr'd an earlier falling-off.
My son, receive my blessing." And the youth
Knelt down beneath the unsteadfast hands and wept ;
And the great-hearted Father blessed him there.
Then when his soul was calmer grown, he said,
" Ah, unto faltering eyes, now half eclipsed
Under the shadow of that ampler world,
How beautiful the footsteps of the youth,
Who, armed with daring thoughts and lofty hopes,
Reverence, persistence and obedient love,
Through the dim courses of bewilder'd men,
Voices that would enchant, affright or mock,
Droops not the eyelid, married in his gaze
To the fair vision that ensnared his soul,
And like a splendor from the inmost heaven,
Illumines and sustains. But ye are yet
The sons of dewy morning in her prime

Of cool slant-glances from thick-fringéd lids.
Her blushing mien will wither in the eye
Of heightening day, the torrid world will crack
With fiery pangs beneath the front of noon,
And the mild evening usher in her balm
With healing lavishment of dews.   Not less
Must ye bear up through all, and must maintain
Your singleness and calmness.   Hardihood
Will spring from wrestling with the stubborn years.
Put on the thews of labor and of joy ;
Strength, which alone in nature may forecast.
Regard me, while I utter what may aid
To raise the future to his lawful height,
And teach your needs.   The son draws from the sire
Ofttimes like fortune with like blood ; so ye,
Seeing ye name me father in your souls,
Like fortune with like wisdom.   This be yours,
As part of somewhat ampler to be yours.
Yoke wisdom unto noble ends of use.
'T is much to know ; but the more daring eye
Not pauses till it speaks a proud ' Behold ! '
And has achieved in visual lineament
That which the mind engendered in itself.
The act, when born, will blend with you anew
To yield you more of being, which ye seek.
He cannot shoot a perfect ray on earth,
The sum of all whose days has been a thought.
Ideül then is idol, not being put
To use, and elemented with the blood
Of the world.   Yet what the loftier faith attains,
Hold fast with calmness and unspeaking lips,

Not doubting. Thus the lowest act will know
The highest purpose, and to it be tuned.
But dwarf not to a blind mechanic round
Of hard performance the majestic scope
Of Duty; knowing that she is a star
Within you, to encircle you with light;
A flower, that, by divinest instincts moved,
Chooses from all the world what best it bears,
And fashions it with light, creative hands,
To her own law of beauty. Work your work.
The world throws open everywhere wide doors
Of invitation. Never can she spare
The toiling hand, the pondering brain, the bright,
High-shooting fancies of her burning youth.
But give her of your best, your best of best ;
Partly defeated in your victories,
Yet ever victors in your vanquishments.

" And Arthur, you perchance will lay your hand
Upon the neck of Turbulence, and tame
His boisterous sport, and ride him to your will ;
And where the smoking bosoms of the world
Shake to the tug of mighty enmities,
Will dip into the thunder, and take part
With God in forging the august event.
This hope is well : and having strongly felt
The master-bias unto action, keep
Endeavor pointed to his lawful goal.
And be not wrenched to sordid uses, born
And cherished by the lean, invidious thought ;
Heroic ardors turned to poisonous smoke.

Nor hope within the easy vale to find
The heavenly flower that blooms in Alpine æries,
Nor yet hope to divorce wisdom from love ;
But seek to temper your achieving hands
With reverence.
             " And Paul, your heart is tuned
To studious moods, and the exalted hour
Of calm and high communings, the intense
Impassioned spiriting of the lonely thought.
Happy, my son, if life shall leave you free
To the delightful, ever gentle power
Of these majestic duties, which we love
To wait upon ; dearest of earthly tasks,
Drawing us like a star that girds her soul
With loveliness in skies of crystalline.
Gladly the hand bends to its proper task.
Gladly the forward mind forecasts the hope
Of liberal labor, reaching out to all
The goals of wisdom by the chosen paths
Of Beauty, and her younger brother, Love.
Sweet is the golden vacancy, whose hours
Of generous toil spread out the willing soul,
Like grapes upon the cancel'd vine, that fill
Their veins with purple from the sun.   To you
The summer skies will yield, with happy grace,
Largess of mellow leisure ; the cool morn,
With swift vivific touch, will fire the breast
With genial courage, and the birds and bees
Will keep you merry through laborious days.
Though many tempting paths invite the foot,
Woo the one Spirit of creative thought,

Who comes most lovely in the shining vest
Of poesy. Wander with her, in heart
Childlike, and what she will reveal, await
With burning soul of large expectancy.

" You Vivian, whom the riddle of the time,
Has sorely plagued with nimble Protean pranks,
Eluding capture, all my being moves
To bless you. O, it is a deep delight
When winter, vanquish'd by the breath of spring,
Strikes all his tents and turns his host to flee,
Wandering in vernal fields to find a flower
Budding on some warm ledge ; a deeper joy
To sailor's eyes, long mocked by cloud and surge,
In the calm hour that tells of storm abating,
High in some glossy folding of the sky,
To catch a star serene in grace and power ;
But sweeter far than these, when the young soul,
Sunk in the abysmal gulfs of self-distrust,
Catching some gleam of what is good and noble,
Shakes off the vapors from his wings, and rolls
The darkness up before him, till he moves
High up through azure plains of light and love.
My son, lose not, I pray you, memory
Of him you spake with in your hour of gloom ;
For from its lifted home my soul will peer,
If this may be, and mark you as you move.
Great is your office, if your hands fail not
In broad outreachings and the secret bond
Creative ; not all captive to the world,
Nor yet unto transcendent glimpses, all,

You shall lay hand on both and make them one ;
By lifting up and luring down, shall blend
The diverse elements in marriage sweet.
And this is greatest. These two strains, when fused
In harmony, are the full life of man."

Long time all hearts were hush, all lips were dumb,
Until he rose and said, " Rise, let us go.
My words are told. Soft slumber laps the world,
And through the misty gleam the muffled sounds
Float slumberous, and the downy airs have fanned
My eyelids into languor. Let us hence.
Death waits me in the valleys, and I go
To meet him as a lover to his bride."

And they arose and passed the wave and stood
Upon the margin of the mount, and saw
The moon lift her wide-smiling argent up
From darkness. And with pencils soft she touched
The broken land, north, south, east, west, and drew
Slow feature after feature into life.
Dim were the master's eyes with tears, the while
He gazed, in solemn farewell long, the paths
Where from his cradle he had gone and come ;
Paths which his mortal steps should know no more.

VII.

When the good man dies,
　Nature feels the drain ;
Heights and depths do sympathize,
　Suns and planets wane.

When the good man dies,
　Nations feel the anguish ;
Thrones are loosened, tumults rise,
　Hearts of heroes languish.

Who shall take his place ?
　None, for none is equal.
Nature not repeats the grace
　Through her endless sequel.

But our fates abide,
　Goodly spheres as any.
Would'st secure thy circle ride,
　Be but one in many.

———◆———

Perfect in age and looking for his end,
The Master sat before the cottage door

Among his kindred in the vale, what hour
The day ebbed slowly from his silent shores.
On one side sat his son ; on one, the wife ;
And at his feet upon her twisted stool,
Edith, who soothed his seam'd and shrivel'd hand
In palms of fairy silkiness ; her heart
Afraid and sorrowful.   Not far, the Three
Were stretched upon the grass, from time to time
Looking on the benignant face they loved,
Best loved of men and most of men revered.
It was an antique chair in which he sat,
Massy and ample, eased with purple softness,
Its cushions lined with homely broideries quaint.
In spires of polished oak high towered the back,
And round the carven arms the lion's mane
Had bristled on his neck a hundred years.
He loved the chair, an heirloom of the house
While two stout sires made white their locks and died.
At his desire the son had wheeled it forth,
Creaking from every joint, as full of groans
As some grey servitor when haply forced
For a light task to quit his chimney-nook.
" Fetch it," he said.   " My father died in it,
And in it, his ; who over the great seas
Brought it from Scotland when his heart was young.
Fling wide the lattice, Edith.   Let him look
On the last hour of whom, a babe, he blessed."
And she flung wide the lattice, and they saw
The great ancestor peering from his frame ;
The port of some bold hunter in the dawn
Of Freedom, striding in the van of things.

And while they sat perusing his ripe age,
He lifted from dim eyes their lids and said,
"My children, it behooves me to pronounce
What last I may ; for I grow weaker now
From pulse to pulse, and can perceive the soul
Begin to stir his plumes for the great flight.
Ah, since in yonder dell the lonely grave
Was rounded, and we planted there the rose,
And missed the perfect fragrance from our lives
Of her that was your mother, now a saint,
The apple of my age is ripe to fall.
Much am I maim'd, not being strong to take,
Nor wise to give. The years, undoing all
They fashioned long ago with many a blow,
Have wrinkled the firm members and bound fast
The will unto the unrevolving wheel
Of his own purposes, and milked the heart
Of those unsleeping currents which it loved.
And yet, and yet another light has shone.
The eve too has its purple with the morn.
Glimpses are mine that never could have pierced
The smoke and tumult of assiduous days.
I am not all forsaken ; for I catch
Some happy visions of an ampler youth
In this most tranquil mirror of my age.
And looking down from this grey verge on that
Which these spent hands have handled, who shall say
That all was sorrow ? Cheated oft of hope,
Bruis'd by defeats and inly-wrung with pangs,
Life has not been a burthen. Though the heart

Has talked with her contrarious forms, has drunk
Her nectar and her gall, and known her moods
Of anger and of dalliance, yet through all,
Though seeming, near, ill passion or worse loss,
Nought that not hatch'd an afterseed of use.
Nothing was vain and nothing overmuch.
But wondrously o'er all was moved a hand,
A rounding hand beneficent, and rich
In compensation ; and the good they took,
The hours brought back a more celestial good.
Thus what the soul achieves so far avails
As gendering oblivion of itself,
A symbol and perpetual furtherance.
And if there be what has not been repaid,
I wait for larger cycles : it will come.
For all the fallings-off we suffer here
Attain their rich completion as we move
From flight to flight, from star to star, far up
The vast serene of never-ending being.
'T is Love that perfects ; his the summing law.
And Love is but the dealing out to each
His share of Beauty, that by single forms
Made perfect, each according to its scope,
The universe may know its harmony,
The manifold be sweetly turned to one.
My children, ye shall fix your hope on Love,
On Him firm base your faith, to Him shall turn
Your thoughts at morn and evening and midday,
And worship Him in secret when ye kneel."

A while he paused for feebleness, then spake ;

" Ye, on whose brow the full meridian glow
Of life reposes in maturest grace,
Telling of cheerful triumphs, bounteous **hearts,**
Ye have not err'd in choosing simple tasks,
Thoughts unperplext by balancings of ill,
Not tempted.   Strive as ye are purely wont.
Finish the purposes ye work upon.
And it shall be that if ye do no wrong,
But taste the world with a wise temperance,
And open to each duty when it knocks,
Conserving with the holy, holy ends,
And know the seasons, careful to provide
What coming days will ask for, ye will **reach**
Serenely and with many thoughts of joy
This brink on which I totter.
                    " O sweet child,
Edith, my darling, in whose soul I hear
That rarest mortal strain, wherein I took
Chiefest delight, prolonged, and those divine
Numbers into your secret being wrought ;
To whom each day is an Eolian change
Into a sweeter music, and the world
Teems like a magic censer whence the joys
Leap forth in gold and purple, may you win
All that the spotless heart can prophesy.
But know that life takes color from the eye,
And the great world smiles with perpetual **charm,**
Because beneath the lovely iris spread
Of your own nature.   Ever keep it pure,
As God is pure.   I know that in your ears
Sounds the new thunder of a mighty sea,

Whereof you know not wholly, though it seem
Within you, partly.   Long time have I marked
The lucent eyelid curtain-in a soul
Perplext with its own womanhood.   Fear not,
O darling daughter, but divinely trust
The beautiful impulsions of your heart,
The calm and holy visions of your mind.
Great Nature has no more beloved task
Then to complete so fair a handiwork.
And him whom you have chosen, while you breathe,
Trust wholly.   For mine eye has seen his soul,
His inmost soul, that it is noble.   Paul,
O love her greatly.   Let no ill divide.
And may Love drink from the celestial fount
Of beauty, which is clearness in the soul.
And feed him on new virtues and fresh graces,
The rose of candor and the bud of hope."

Now from the altar of the fading day
The embers shot a dying flicker faint ;
And all his spirit mounted, hovering
About the brightening face of that fair star,
Lovliest star the jewel-wearing west
Puts on anight, the mildest-eyed, that lay
Within the elbow of a cloud and smiled
Sweet as a babe ; whose glow for the last time
He drank to feed his heart and soothe his eyes.
And cheerly fell his accents, as he said,
" O mine own star, belov'd above all orbs
That pace the courts of God with brows serene,
Burn in me and inspire me as I die.

Shoot down a summoning welcome that will tempt
This halting spirit through the door it holds
Ajar.   For largely from your fount I took
In days that felt the shadow and the pain,
Trusting your hallowed comfort, winning thence
Constant thanksgiving and perennial calm.
Yea, I have known you as a guardian force,
A genius by my side through good and ill,
My star of fate.   No weariness makes wan
Your glorious eye, nor stains of travel mar
Your garments.   I am gladdened and renewed
By this proud port and unabated will."

He bowed his head and many memories,
Saddest and sweetest of his mortal hour,
Came to him through the falling twilight, touched,
And touching, like to wrestling angels, loosed
His sinews.   And the group that watched him feared
His end was on him, but he said, "Not yet."
And somewhat his cheek brightened as he spoke,
" My sons, newly adopted, 't is my hope
My mountains have been liberal hosts to you.
Come often, when my bones are turned to dust.
They will not fail in bounty, and will wake
Some fond remembrance of my love for you,
A solace and a strengthening when ye
Go down into the semblance of the world
And thread the misty alleys of your lives.

Anon the transient lustre of his cheek
Died into pallor native to his years.

All waited breathless, and he lifted up
The trembling hands and, faltering somewhat,
      breathed
An ample benediction, as beseemed
So old and great a heart.   An hour they sat
In utter stillness there.   But when in heaven
The vesper star was tottering on the verge
Of the dim world, his spirit on its perch
A little fluttered.   Faintly then he said,
" Farewell : my soul is summoned.   I must go.
Edith, my darling, kiss me."   And she rose
And stooped upon his breast and kissed his lips
That gave no answering greeting, but were chill.
Yet in his eyes she caught, though faint and far,
The smiling of his ghost, now half withdrawn
From the slow-darkening windows of the sense.
Then she sat down and hid her face and wept.
Her sorrow deepened and she wept aloud.
And when the dying signal of the star
Shone out and vanished, to his breast he bowed
His face, all clothed with august quietude,
Seeming to hide serenest ponderings.
And on the bosom of unspeakable Love
His spirit drooped its shining head like it,
That perfect flower, bending its petals fair,
Heavy with light, stooping from weight of dreams,
Upon the glowing parterre of the west,
Hesper.

         All stilly wept, till Vivian rose,
And looking on his lifeless master said,
" O thou great Heart !   O largest, wisest, best,

Most royal-fashioned, godlike man of men!
The world was never great enough for you,
And this vast love that templed in you here.
But ever you conversed with loftier worlds ;
Melodious spheres and fairer than our stars,
Clothed with a light not born from any sun,
But which creates itself from year to year.
Without you I had never known the worth,
The loveliness and majesty of man.
Without you I had never known of Love.
O holy be your ashes and the spot
Holy, where they shall rest in peace, among
The flowers that knew you and the birds that knew,
And these fair hills that loved you as their son.
And often will I slip the noisy world
And come, a duteous pilgrim, to your grave,
And wander all the paths you loved so well,
That memory of your greatness, oft renewed,
May spur the bating heart and quicken it
To hope, to toil, to suffer and endure."

He ceased.   The stars shone brighter.   The dews
    fell.
The world through all her sloping vales was still ;
Only were heard two katydids that sang
In answer on the summit of an oak.

www.ingramcontent.com/pod-product-compliance
Lightning Source LLC
Chambersburg PA
CBHW030610040726
47497CB00008B/2923